WORLDSHIFTER

Author's Dedication:
For Deborah, who builds our world

WORLDSHIFTER

Paul Di Filippo

NewCon Press
England

First published in the UK April 2021 by
NewCon Press
41 Wheatsheaf Road,
Alconbury Weston,
Cambs, PE28 4LF

NPN003 (limited edition hardback)
NPN004 (paperback)

10 9 8 7 6 5 4 3 2 1

ISBN:

978-1-912950-86-7 (hardback)
978-1-912950-87-4 (paperback)

Cover layout and design by Ian Whates

Typesetting and editorial meddling by Ian Whates
Text layout by Ian Whates

One

Shipbreaker

"If this was what death was, somebody ought to care."
– *Earthblood*, by Keith Laumer and Rosel George Brown

A craggy, jagged mountain fell slowly through the sky.

Attended by a flock of Class D Hagfish pilot ships, their coruscant supportive fields overlapping the larger vessel, the dead hulk of another retired starliner descended toward the Shipbreakers' Yard on Asperna. Possessing no discernible symmetry, the machicolated and turretted starcraft was a conglomeration of protuberances and ports, pods and pavilions, so ugly it forced the viewer to concede new notions of beauty. Its space-pitted, many-textured surfaces bespoke millennia of interstellar service.

Occulting Asperna's Least Sun, the dropping starliner robbed each individual in the crowd below of a single shadow. A vast horde of ragged workers, the crowd featured one or two representatives from the Yard's management. Apart from their finer clothing and lack of visible cruft, these overseers could also be recognised by their attendant swarms of majestatics.

The workers and executives had arrayed themselves randomly along a wide sloping beach of firm-packed sand, facing the water. On either extreme of the gathering lay vast hard-surfaced staging areas for the upcoming deconstruction, dotted with tools and agravitic lifters and cradles which would soon receive components gutted from the newest salvage prize. The shoreline was stained with exotic industrial fluids that had killed off all vegetation and tinted in oily chromatics the waters themselves. At several docks bobbed scores of dirty utilitarian slab-sided watercraft used to ferry workers out to the ship-corpse, their lifting units deactivated.

Behind the onlookers stretched inland the nameless collection of hovels and shanties, shacks and huts, warehouses and refectories, barrooms and brothels, laced together by muddy paths, all of which the shipbreakers simply called home. At the very edge of the water and wading into the shallows, a vast system of tall baffles and shunts – a diamond labyrinth – stood poised to deal with the imminent surge that would accompany the ponderous settling of the starliner into the sea.

Now the descent of the falling mountain and its host of attendants slowed even more dramatically. The liner that had once cruised like a queen among the worlds of the Indrajal seemed to hover unmoving in the atmosphere. But ever so timidly the Least Sun emerged crescentwise from behind its upper rim, indicating a slight actual progress toward berthing.

The lower edge of the liner lipped the waves. The Hagfishes pulled their fields steadily upward from contact with the rising water, not wishing to dissipate power by lifting cubic metres of sea needlessly. As their fields shifted off the centre of the big's ship's mass, the little craft had to strain to maintain the equilibrium of their prize. Soon, judging by the strobing moire patterns, they would have to let their capture go.

When the ocean had swallowed the bottom third of the liner, a dark architectonic iceberg, the pilot ships cut their fields entirely.

The resulting tidal surge whooshed shoreward, smashed the baffles, then dissipated in a chaos of foam and spume and a noise like the manifestation of a deva.

From the crowd ascended a lusty cheer. Here was work aplenty for the next several months. Fat profits, to be sure, for the Shipyard's owner – the enigmatic and seldom-glimpsed Horseface known as Bright Tide Rising – but enough scraps, at least, to sustain the meagre lives of the breakers themselves.

And, as always, the dream –

Perhaps one of the breakers would even strike it rich, finding something on board that earned its discoverer a bonus. Hefty by comparison with the regular day rates, these incentive payments represented the smallest fraction of what Bright Tide Rising would resell the prizes for.

But the breakers were in no position to bargain or complain.

Klom turned to the woman at his side. Sorrel's buttery face was sheened with salty spray blown back from the collision of tide and baffles, and her auburn hair was damp. A smear of neglected grease grimed one hinge of her jaw; scavenged O-rings served her as bracelets, and an unredeemable chunk of fused gold circuitry spotwelded to a clasp hung from one small earlobe.

Klom lifted a blunt-fingered hand big enough to palm Sorrel's head like a gameball. The back of his hand was tessellated with the latest cruft, a mica-like substance that evolved out of Klom's epidermal cells and flaked off regularly. The cruft had come in on the Snuffler ship they dismantled some months ago, and as yet the Yard's curanderos had no remedy for the exogenous affliction. With a forefinger large as the nozzle of a watercutter, Klom swiped moisture from the skin underneath Sorrel's green, horizontally slitted left eye and down over her sharp cheekbone.

"You got wet."

Sorrel glared up at Klom, who towered above her much as the floating ship now towered over the crowd, even at the remove of a kilometre. Her throaty voice registered exasperation. "Big news, you dumb two-strand! We all did."

"Oh." Klom raised the hem of his tattered coarse shirt, revealing a midriff packed with muscle and striated with more cruft. He dried his own rugged face. "I didn't even feel the spray. I was busy thinking about my mother."

Sorrel snorted. "Your mother! You haven't even seen the woman in ten years. I'm sure she would have forgotten that you even exist, if it weren't for the money you send."

"Maybe this ship will make us rich, Sorrel. Enough for you and me and my mother too. We could go back to my village and all three of us could live together. You'd like living in Chaulk, I know it. There's a lake there –"

"Oh, my deva! I've heard about Lake Zawinul so often I'm starting to develop gills! And what makes you think I'd go with you to your stinking little home village even if you were rich? I used to be a city girl, you know, before I had the misfortune to end up here. Can Chaulk compete with the Whispering Gardens of Lustron?"

Utter incomprehension transformed Klom's massive features into a mask of hurt confusion. "But Sorrel, we love each other."

"So you keep telling me."

Klom shook himself as if dispelling a cloud of the gnats that arose in the springtime from the stagnant marshes bordering the Yard. Then, forsaking words, he enwrapped Sorrel with one arm and hugged her to him. Her olive-drab shift bunched up on one hip. Klom's smile was holed here and there by missing teeth.

"Ow! Let me go, you big idiot!"

"Hey now, what's this? Assault on a lady? Shall I be forced to give you a good thrashing, you monster?"

Weaving through the throng came a lean man with coppery skin and sandy hair, dressed in what passed for finery among the breakers: clean, albeit ragged white blouse and trews. A wispy mustache draped his upper lip. Taller than Sorrel, he still seemed small in comparison with Klom. Closing with Klom and Sorrel, the newcomer began darting and feinting, tossing mild jabs at the giant.

Klom released Sorrel, and laughed in such a titanic manner that the nearest bystanders winced. "Airey! Where were you? You missed the landing!"

Airey ceased his shadowboxing and shook Klom's hand. "Deva bless you, Klom, that cruft's hideous! Don't you have any gloves?"

Klom examined his hands as if seeing them for the first time. "No gloves fit me."

"Nonsense! I'll get you a pair that fits somehow." Airey turned to Sorrel and briefly embraced her, bestowing a kiss on her forehead. "Any damage to the fleshy goods? No? Very well, but let me know if your reputation needs avenging." Sorrel laughed, her bell-like tones generating more pleasant notice from those nearby than Klom's robust guffaws.

"Airey, you make everyone laugh," Klom said.

"Too bad I can't convince old Right Tight Raisin to pay me for such services. Yard comedian, that's a role I could enjoy! Instead, I have to labour in the drainage pits like some unskilled kilobase. And if beauty were money, Sorrel wouldn't have to slave on the sorting line. Oh well, that's life."

Klom scratched his head through a thick mat of black hair. "Maybe this new ship will bring us all good luck."

"Ah, that's the very reason I sought you out, Klom. I did not miss the landing at all. I was standing as close to the overseers as I could get, while the ship came down. Those lousy terabases and four-strands are damnably suspicious of eavesdroppers, though! It was all I could do to avoid rousing their majestatics."

"You didn't take any chances, did you?" asked Sorrel, looking alarmed.

Airey patted her hand. "Not at all. I have no desire to be drilled through the heart by an angry busybee, believe me! But I was able to overhear the high and mighty ones discussing the origin of this ship. It's a Vixen craft. Most recently made the circuit among Bastiaan, Meuse and Greengage for centuries. But it's much older than that. Parts of it were decommissioned over a thousand years ago. That's where I'd head first if I were you, Klom. Deva knows what goodies you'll find there!"

Klom considered the information, ruminating over it in his slow, stolid fashion. Any idea introduced into Klom's brain met with a laborious reception, but frequently he ground a notion to a finer intellectual dust than the more quick-witted Airey ever could, with surprising results.

"I'll do that, Airey. Anything special I should look for?"

"Oh, I don't know... What about the Book of Forgetting?"

Sorrel laughed, but sourly this time. "Why not hope to find a globe of Mazarine isinglass, or a Ledan swanrobe or a map to the treasures of Mount Sumeru while you're at it?" Here she broke mockingly into a snatch of song: "'The fields of pleasure, the seas of love/Heavenly eyes that peer from above....' And how would anyone even recognise the mythical Book of Forgetting?"

"Oh, if half of what's said about it is true, I suspect the finder would quickly realise what they'd found. The legends are evocative, though not precise. The Book is nothing less than the universal anodyne for all our mortal suffering —"

Suddenly the crowd surged forward en masse, breaking around Klom's immovable bulk, which protected his companions as well.

"What's happening?" asked Klom.

"I assume the marabouts are about to invoke a deva to bless the proceedings," said Airey.

"Lift me up," Sorrel said, and I'll tell you what I can see."

Klom's hands encircled Sorrel's torso just as her O-ring bracelets encircled her wrist. His fingers and thumbs met across her span. In half a second she stood on his shoulders, her sandaled feet finding plenty of purchase on Klom's broad frame, while he braced her behind her thighs. Canopying her hands, Sorrel shielded her eyes against the triple sunlight.

"Yes, I see it all now. Several marabouts are riding a lifter out to the ship. Oh, how beautiful their robes are, billowing in the wind! Oops, one's lost his mitre! They've stopped now, not far from the ship. They're making the sacrifice. I think they're using a Redskull ox." A tremulous bellow cut short drifted across the waters. "Now they're feeding power to the prayer wheels. Get ready for the boomtube –"

Airey covered his ears, as did Sorrel. Klom seemed unconcerned, but in any case did not cease supporting Sorrel.

If the might of the tidal surge hitting the baffles had produced a noise akin to the collapse of a small house, then the manifestation of the deva's boomtube generated a soundwave resembling the demolition of one of Voyle's cloudscraper towers. The whole crowd staggered backward, with some losing their footing. Klom barely rocked, while he kept Sorrel anchored.

Now above the floating ship hung the deva: a silvery distortion in the air in which the minds of lesser beings discerned varying images, depending on both physiology and cultural conditioning.

The majority of sapients in the galaxy – Humans, Foambones, Weepers, Hyenas, Gadabouts, Crickets, Leatherheads, Cygnets, as well as a thousand others and all their miscegenous offspring – encoded their genomes in some variation of DNA: two helical strands of nucelotides on the order of three billion basepairs. But there were higher orders of natural beings as well, those whose longer evolutionary histories had achieved more. Their genomes consisted of four, six, or even eight strands, featuring trillions of basepairs. These terabase beings exhibited emergent properties, sophistications of mind and body unattainable by the two-strands and gigabases.

The devas were sentients who had bootstrapped themselves entirely out of conventional spacetime thanks to their cellular complexity: decastranders, yotta- and zettabases. The subtle cosmic fields that supported life simply kicked the devas up to a different quantum level of existence.

Sorrel shivered atop Klom. "I see a Trundler Demon. This is a bad omen."

"Nonsense," said Airey. "I can plainly discern the smiling face of a Hovaness Lamb. Nothing could be a better sign. Klom, what do you see?"

Klom did not speak immediately. "I – I don't know the name for what I'm seeing."

"Can you describe it?"

"It's – it forgives everything."

Airey made a dismissive noise. "Oh, that's helpful, all right."

A bolt of silver energy lanced out from the deva and splattered across the ship: a token of beneficence. A joyous shout went up from the crowd at this blessing. Then the deva silently snapped out of their ontological plane.

"Okay, Klom, you can put me down now."

Klom complied effortlessly. Airey tugged straight his best white tunic, which had been disarrayed by the boomtube's blast, and said, "Well, I think this event calls for a drink. Shall we go to Thrash's for a flagon of toadchunder?"

"Who's paying?" asked Sorrel.

Airey clapped Klom on the shoulder. "Why, Klom of course. He's the one who saw the unknowable face of the deva. He's the one who's going to get rich!"

The gangboss for Klom's shift was a Quetzal from Muntjac, named Rapaille. The amputation of Rapaille's wings necessitated by a clumsy curandero after a barroom brawl had long ago left the avianoform ill-tempered and unforgiving. As meagre compensation for his lost wings, Rapaille spent every last spare taka and paisa to adorn his priapic cockscomb with a variety of gaudy baubles. Today, setting out for their first foray to the Vixen hulk, Rapaille wore several sparkling garnets and a lozenge of nightmare amber piercing his fleshy ruff.

Aboard one of the wallowing, unroofed ocean transports, still docked, Rapaille marshalled his workers, a motley pack of hard-limbed bruisers representing a dozen heterogenous races. Mounting one of the grimy seats to command more attention, Rapaille commenced a small speech. His beak clacked between syllables, and his narrow orange tongue stabbed the air.

"Listen closely, you scuzz-buckets! This ship has already been partially stripped by its former owners. They've taken most of the furnishings and fixtures. You won't find any old nesting materials to sniff, nor any dainty female undergarments to hug to your bosom."

An anonymous voice called out, "How about wings? Any chance of glomming a pair of those onboard?"

Rapaille scrunched his beady eyes and gurgled wordlessly, before regaining his self-control. "Quiet! The next wisecrack will earn someone a lost shift! Pay attention! It is equally unlikely you'll discover any valuable personal trinkets or artwork, although I don't rule out a few overlooked nanosculptures or parasite jewellery. So you might as well just forget about such easy booty. Any individual performance rewards will come from the neat and speedy accumulation of well-known structures. We're after control ganglia, matter-modems and entertainment nodes, for instance. Nexial splitters pay well too. Several teams have already been dispatched to handle the disentanglers and decoherers. Other groups have been assigned the bridge. But aside from those areas, we have free access to the rest of the ship. Our goal is to finish over the next few months at the same time as the others, so that we can all move on to breaking up the hull itself. Do you all have your downloaded ship schematics?"

Several breakers held aloft their industrial-grade readers, battered boxes good for little more than displaying pre-formatted audiovisual files. No ensouled devices were to be found on Asperna, at least among the lower castes.

"All right, then! Take your seats, and we'll be off!"

Before Rapaille could step off his own bench, Klom pushed forward through his fellows to confront the gangboss. Strapped across Klom's massive torso were various prybars, clamps, spreaders, holdfasts, desiccant packs and other tools. Slung in a holster at one hip was his bulky watercutter.

Even atop his seat, Rapaille found himself staring at Klom's chest rather than his face, until he raised his scale-rimmed eyes. "Yes, our big empty-headed man-ape from Chaulk. What do you want?"

"Are we allowed to go into the decommissioned areas?"

Rapaille let out a tweet of amazement. "The decommissioned areas? What are you interested in? Dust and bones? Faded signage and outmoded tech? Slavering senescent slop? That's all you'll find there!"

Klom blinked once, then said, "Are we allowed to go into the decommissioned areas?"

The Quetzal screeched in frustration, his wing stubs twitching beneath his embroidered shirt. "Go anyplace you want, you unreasoning curdled egg! But you'll never earn more than base pay if you persist in this foolish strategy. And my own bonuses will fall accordingly!"

Klom said, "I will be going into the decommissioned areas then." He sat down, occupying two seats.

Muttering, Rapaille signalled liftoff to the transport's pilot – a diminutive Melungeon with one tendril wrapped around a joystick and five others free for the separate controls. The transport lost mass until it floated half a metre above the waves. Surging forward through a channel opened in the baffles, the craft headed toward the Vixen ship. The Great Sun and the Lesser Sun raised the temperature of the air to a comfortable, shirtsleeve level. By the time the Least Sun arose, rendering the muggy atmosphere tropical, the breakers would be taking their lunch deep within the hulk.

The crossing of the kilometre of open water by Klom's craft and its mates resembled the engulfment of a school of minnows by a leviathan. The minor-city-sized disabled starcruiser – with the waterline halfway up its height, and its lower portions resting on the seabed – thrust out artificial peninsulas and lesser promontories. Once into its shadow and embrace, the transports assumed the insignificance of ticks on the hide of a Dominikono widestrider. Additionally, the ancient interstellar vessel seemed to be reradiating all the immeasurable chill it had accumulated over millennia of high vacuum service.

It would take the gangs nearly a year to finish stripping the interior of the craft, and another six months to disassemble the hull. Of course, the whole process could have been accomplished in a fraction of that time by employing sufficient swarms of self-replicating majestatics. But such technologies – along with ensouled machines – were forbidden to anyone not at least a fourstrand. And the fourstrands and other galactic elites were both relatively small in number and disdainful of performing any such 'labour', even distanced by layers of autonomic supervisors. With the fecund and subservient twostrands so handy, it only made sense to keep them profitably occupied.

The Yards at Asperna not only saw ships come in, but also go out, as saleable constituent pieces. Brokers arrived and departed continuously, both from offplanet and from other parts of Asperna, leaving with cargoes for a hundred thousand destinations. Workers in the warehouse and sales end of the Yards felt their positions to be superior to the gritty, effortful tasks of the breakers and sorters, and a rough caste system existed, further fragmented into various levels according to the perceived crudity of assignments.

Klom's boat arrived at a sloping paw of the inorganic leviathan. Far, far above them, a different portion of the starliner

11

formed a concave roof. A shoulder of the starliner constituted a distant wall running roughly parallel to the arm. A chaotic illumination came into this partial gallery as sunlight refracted from the bouncing sea.

The Melungeon shut down the lifting units, then secured the transport by a cable to a handy U-bar on the Vixen vessel. The breakers utilised the fractally porous surface of the starcraft's skin as handholds and toeholds to climb up several gently sloping metres of wall, their tools racketing against each other. Once aboard this small leg of the starliner – broad enough to host a ballgame – they waited for Rapaille's commands.

"Follow me, you wittolds! The nearest port is just a few minutes' walk in this direction."

The paw sloped upward, the roof sloped down, and the shoulder angled in, rendering the passage more tunnel-like the further the breakers progressed.

Klom marched at the head of the line, looking about with a kind of patient curiosity. He had taken apart a dozen ships so far in his career at the Yards, and he fully expected to take apart a few dozen more before he got too old for the work. Each ship possessed its own personality. Klom assumed that by the time he was done breaking down this vessel, he would know good-sized portions of it as intimately as he knew his mother's house in Chaulk. Paradoxically, the ship would no longer then exist to be known. Such conundrums did not bother Klom.

Faded Vixen script, each character tall as a man, ran across this segment of the deck. Klom turned to the breaker next to him, a blue-haired, ice-skinned fellow named Nyerephar, a mixed-breed Human and Pinemarten from Frostholm. Nyerephar had a reputation as an intellectual, given his predilection for offshift downloading into his reader of novels of interspecies romance, many of which originated with the Vixens.

"What do these words say, 'Phar?"

Nyerephar smoothed his long jutting whiskers before replying. "It could be the ship's name. Yes, that's it, I'm sure. This is the ship's name."

"And what is the ship's name, 'Phar?"

"'Caution Discharge Zone'"

"Thank you for telling me this."

Soon the breakers arrived at the port. Standing outside in front of the entrance was an enormous matter-modem: a cube with one mirrored face.

Delivered earlier from the Yards, the teleportation device stood ready to receive any unliving object carved from the ship. Its mates, tunable at will, stood ashore, near the sorting lines. Very useful devices, integral to the functioning of most economies of the Indrajal, the matter-modems were subject to two major inconvenient limitations. They only operated over planetary distances, and they were death to anything living that attempted transit.

Now the matter-modem, sensing their presence, activated itself. Fed from the other end, a fleet of lifting sledges came through the mirror face. Each breaker stepped up to take a floating sledge for carrying booty.

Rapaille triggered a Vixen wall control marked by a new slash of red spray paint, and the port hobermanned open. The black interior of the powerless ship beckoned like the afterlife. The breakers lowered their miners' lamps onto their foreheads and switched them on, flooding the scene with actinic light.

"Rendezvous back here at twenty-nine hundred hours. And remember! This was a luxury vessel intended to pamper its patrons, not a Scryer dreadnought bristling with weaponry. Nonetheless, you can die just as swiftly from a falling girder as you can from an antipersonnel wasp!"

One by one, with Klom leading the way, the breakers stepped inside.

Klom grunted hoarsely as he completed his climb. Sweat rivuleted his skin, and a musty odour compounded of stale lubricants and malnourished organic units pumping out ketones made every breath an exercise in disgust.

The ship schematics on his reader informed him that the ladder he had just topped ran for a kilometre and a half in a narrow shaft slicing through innumerable decks. The swiftest way to the closest decommissioned area, the ladder had seemed a gift when Klom stood at its base. But now, as he laboured to catch his breath on a platform above 1500 metres of nothingness, the ladder appeared more like a poisoned fruit. Even Klom's work-hardened muscles quivered from the gruelling ascent. Had his lifter fit into the narrow shaft, the ascent would have been trivial. Now, though, Klom was fatigued before he even began whatever labours awaited him.

Klom broke out his water bottle and a beancake. The water, sterilised by passage through a matter-modem, still retained the distasteful taints of decay and the metallic flavours of the marshes from which it was drawn. But this was the only drinking water available to the bustee-dwellers of Klom's caste. After so many years in the Yard, Klom was inured to the taste. But he still recalled the pure waters of Lake Zawinul with each sip.

After consuming the last crumb of beancake, Klom stood and faced away from the shaft. The door at the end of the platform presented itself as his next challenge. He looked for some control similar to the one Rapaille had used outside, but no such mechanism showed. It did not take Klom long to decide to cut his way through.

The watercutter hanging from his belt was a simple pistol-shaped device with a second grip up front for two-handed use. Klom had wrapped tape around the butts for firmer purchase. He fitted a pair of scratched plastic goggles over his eyes, braced himself against a convenient strut, then triggered the cutter.

Out of its nozzle leaped a needle-thin jet of water possessing the destructive power of any stream of collimated subatomic particles, without any inconvenient radiation.

The closed end of the watercutter's barrel was a tiny matter-modem synced to another resting in a deep-sea trench where the water was at several dozen atmospheres of pressure. Only breakers of Klom's raw strength could handle this device, whose light weight and inexhaustibility were unmatched by any other cutting tool.

Klom inscribed a crude circle in the wall just big enough for him to crawl through. A salty mist enveloped him, making his footing and handholds tenuous. Practically at his elbow, the echoing drop into space awaited his first slip. But he coolly persisted. Finally finished, he kicked the circle of metal inward. Gaily coloured fluids from severed conduits dribbled into the opening, where once, when the ship was under power, they might well have gushed. Klom squirmed through this mild dribble without concern.

On the far side, he found himself in a giant auditorium or ballroom or refectory, whose vast confines his headlamp barely illuminated. This room had been in active use right up until the end, but the decommissioned area lurked just beyond its remote wall.

Klom crossed the wide floorspace, the beam of his lamp picking out various columns and stubs of fixtures and some discarded artifacts which to a less ambitious breaker would have represented adequate salvage. But with Airey's tactics fixed firmly in his mind, Klom zeroed in on the mysteries of the long-sealed chambers.

A little searching revealed a door concealed behind a sagging arras that depicted the hunting of some spiny beast by a party of Vixens, the bushy tails of the hunters plaited with colourful streamers. The door – sealed with a blobby gasket of silicone – boasted a still-active glo-sign, but not in Vixen script. Half the letters in the independently powered message were dead with age, while the rest exhibited only a marginal brightness. But Klom could not have read the warning or advice even if active, so ancient and foreign was the script. Without any hesitation, he simply cut his way past it.

The space on the far side of the door, a corridor, was proportioned for creatures somewhat smaller than Klom. The big man had to hunch as he advanced. Dust lay thickly underfoot, and the air smelled of the slow disintegration of unnatural materials. The walls of the corridor were etched with shallow glyphs, as if the beings who once traversed it had relied on tactile clues more than visual ones.

Some years ago, Klom had helped disassemble a Pingpank ship that featured similar carven icons, although much cruder. But the Pingpank had been extinct for five hundred years, and at the time of their disappearance had represented the degenerate offspring of a much more sophisticated race, the Marchwardens. If this were Marchwarden text, then the decommissioned segment of the ship had last been occupied over a millennium ago. Without any exo-inputs, even generations of invisible repair majestatics would be reaching the end of their preservation efforts.

Open arched doorways began to appear. Klom cautiously poked his head through each one. Most of the chambers were of moderate size, and easily scannable for booty. In one such, Klom found several crystal eggs harbouring strange animated scenes flickering wispily in their centres. These he placed in a carrying pouch. But the majority of the chambers were utterly bare. Klom began to suspect that Rapaille's harsh words held more accuracy than Airey's optimistic encouragements. Nonetheless, he continued his search.

The corridor dead-ended at another door. Klom saltily sliced through it, the runoff from his cutter turning the dust at his feet to a thin river of mud.

Pushing the cut circle of metal clangingly inward, he was met by a gust of pungent atmosphere. He stepped warily inside.

Instantly Klom knew he had found a vivarium.

From the walls of the tall, extensive chamber hung a variety of suspensor-sacs, all of them, sadly, in various stages of decomposition. Klom walked over to the nearest such: the withered reticulated vesicle ripped apart easily under his big hands with a noise like shredding a few dozen thicknesses of paper, and a shower of skeletal fragments fell out, clattering noisily on the floor.

Klom kicked the bones in frustration. So far he had wasted nearly half a shift and discovered nothing to justify his efforts. At this rate, retirement with Sorrel to Chaulk seemed destined never to be more than a dream.

Wearily, Klom sat down and took out another beancake.

The majestatic that appeared hovering over his beancake resembled a thumb-sized golden bee. Klom jerked back, dropping the food. The majestatic levitated the cake and flew ponderously off with it.

Klom jumped up and followed.

Clinging to the far side of a massive pillar, a live suspensor-sac served as the focus of a thick swarm of shining majestatics. The agravitic attendants ranged in size from dust particles to hummingbirds. They wreathed the sac in a life-supporting cloud. Already Klom's lunch was being disassembled into its constituent nutrients to benefit the sac.

Why this one vesicle had survived, Klom did not know. Perhaps it had sent taps into the support pillar, finding necessary sustenance elsewhere, in the active portions of the *Caution Discharge Zone*. But whatever anomaly was responsible for extending its life beyond its mates, the sac represented a potential treasure.

Inside, a living mature being awaited rebirthing. For some unknown period, the metabolism of the concealed creature had

17

been stepped down to nearly flatline levels, with interior majestatics tending to various cellular repairs as necessary. Given adequate resources, the upper time limit on sac containment had never been established.

Klom advanced on the sac, then stopped. He could not simply rip it open, he realised. How was he to get the vesicle to awaken and safely discharge its patient?

Filled with a fierce wanting, Klom hung his head and cudgled his thoughts for a solution.

Suddenly his vision was obscured by a shifting haze. A portion of the turbulent majestatic swarm had englobed his head.

"Please," said Klom aloud, "deliver your burden to me. This ship is dead. We are going to chop it up. Your charge will die."

Spinning in arcane patterns, the majestatics seemed to consider Klom's request, before rejoining the parent cloud.

Instantly, the vesicle began to undergo changes. Veins throbbed athwart its surface, swaths of livid colour flowed across it like storms across a gas-giant planet, and a musky, urinous odour arose off it.

A split developed along the bottom ridge of the vesicle, widening quickly. The next instant clotted crimson and purple fluids gushed out, splashing Klom's workboots, followed by the plopping thud of a body hitting the floor.

Klom hastened over and squatted down beside the form, roughly one third as big as Klom himself. It resembled no sapient race he had ever seen.

The creature's head was an oblate boulder pebbled over with muffin-sized mounds. It had two eyes, now lidded, a blunt snout with flaring nostrils, and jowl-concealed jaws. A kind of skin-covered cartilaginous tuning-fork arrangement projected from its forehead. No ears were visible. Its keg-like body boasted four chunky legs, the paws showing blunt claws. Its hide was brown velvety skin wrinkled like a cortex. A pair of vestigial hands stuck out at its shoulders. No tail interrupted its hindquarters.

The being was struggling to draw breath. Klom gripped it by the scruff of its neck with one hand, lifting its weighty head, then levered open its unresisting jaws with the other. He swabbed out a jellylike mass from its throat, then put his face to the creature's wet face and began exchanging breaths with it.

After a minute, the beast could breathe on its own. It opened its eyes, limpid grey pools. Klom fell into the creature's gaze, losing all sense of self for a moment. When he had recovered, he asked, "Can you speak? Are you all right?" The creature said nothing, but tried to stand. Its legs gave way beneath it, however, and it collapsed back into the afterbirth.

Klom picked up the creature and set out to retrace his steps.

At the platform where the ladder began, he lashed the beast to his chest with a net of bungee cords, so that its head rested below Klom's chin.

Klom commenced the descent.

Halfway down, his muscles spasming, Klom thought he might not be able to complete the climb.

A giant tongue stropped his face.

Klom found the strength to go on.

The interior of Thrash's shabeen was illuminated only by a few worthless lighting fixtures scavenged from a variety of ships, and powered off a rack of biomass fuelcells. The patchy, sputtering radiance formed many shadowy nooks where drinkers could sit and conspire, consummating the mingy deals that constituted the primitive economy of the bustee-dwellers in the Yard. The furniture of the dirt-floored barroom was similarly ill-sorted, a collection of spraddle-legged chairs and tables, and the occasional stained, bedraggled lounge for those customers whose anatomy precluded chairs. At the bar, the best-lit area, a row of stools with fragments of flooring still attached rested hard by the stacked packing crates separating Thrash from his customers.

19

Thrash's heritage included Slow Loris and Peluche genes, rendering him a shaggy ursinoid with huge eyes. All the tap-handles and liquor jugs had been customised for his broad paws. The mugs all sported wide grips as well.

Sorrel needed both hands to lift her glass. She raised her drink and sipped, then made a face before plonking the mug back on the rickety table.

"What sour piss this is! How I wish I had a glass of Tancredi nectar."

Klom drained his own dark brew with evident satisfaction, then wiped his mouth with the back of his crufty hand.

Sorrel winced. "Deva, Klom! I have to kiss those lips once in a while!"

Looking down at his flaking hand, Klom said, "But Sorrel, we know this cruft's not contagious. The curandero said so. Once it finds a host, it stops looking for others. It's worked its way right into me, though, adopting lots of my genes into itself. That's what makes it so hard to get rid of."

"That's no matter. I still prefer not to have those patches rubbed all over me, or to come in contact with certain parts of you. You're just lucky the cruft stopped at your waist."

Klom smiled dreamily. "Tonight we'll doublecheck its progress."

Sorrel stuck out her vividly pink tongue. "If you can spare a minute for me, now that you've got a new friend. Or if there's a centimetre of space left in your crib."

Klom looked down at his feet.

The creature from the *Caution Discharge Zone* lay peacefully sleeping, one forepaw folded over the other beneath its chin. Drool snailed down the side of its face to darken the dirt. Its unlaboured breathing gently rasped the stale air within the shabeen.

Reaching down, Klom fondly skritched the beast's scalp around its fleshy forklike appendage. The rhythm of the creature's breathing deepened in a contented fashion. "Use his name, Sorrel, please. You know I gave him a name. Call him Tugger, please."

"Tugger! Ridiculous! Why 'Tugger', anyhow?"

"I found out he likes to play that way. You should see him pull on a rope. He can put up a real tussle."

"And why 'he'?" I certainly didn't see any bollocks on him when you trotted him around for everyone to admire."

"I don't know. I just feel Tugger's male."

Sorrel waved her arms about in frustration. "I give up! You get first crack at a potential treasure trove, and all you come away with is an ugly pet! This is so typical for you, Klom. You're just too dumb to grab the main chance, even when it's right under your nose."

Klom looked hurt. "There was nothing valuable in that decommissioned area, Sorrel. At least as far as I looked. But I stopped when I found Tugger. I had to get him out of there. The atmosphere was bad for him. And he perked up right away, once we were outside in the fresh air. But I shared the money from the crystal eggs with you, didn't I? Ten taka and sixty paisa. That's something, isn't it?"

"Birdscratch! Someone with your experience should be hauling in much more. Tomorrow, I expect you to pick another decommissioned area and make a big strike!"

"But I already found something very valuable, Sorrel. Tugger! Just look at him. What a character! He makes me smile, just like Airey does. Who could ask for anything more? Anyway, I figure if I concentrate on ripping out the old Vixen equipment like everyone else, I can make a steadier pay. No, I'm not going back to any of the decommissioned areas. The odds are too slim."

"What's this, what's this? Abandoning my advice! I'm hurt! Truly I am!"

Airey dropped down onto an empty ladderback chair. He wore a shirt that proclaimed with glowing threads support for his favourite ballteam, the Alavoine Tumblers. His bronze face was slicked with sweat, rendering his moustache a limp strip of furze. Even hours after Final Sunset, the air retained a surplus of enervating heat.

Signalling to Thrash for a drink, Airey resumed his chiding. "So, you're letting one little setback discourage you, Klom? I had thought much higher of you."

"Setback? What setback?"

Airey dug a toe of his sandal into Tugger's side, provoking a mild grunt and a shifting away by the beast. "This worthless thing! Now you have another mouth to feed. Have you considered that?"

Klom remained positive. "I can't get Tugger to eat anything yet. All he does is drink a little water. And he seems to do that just to please me. He just doesn't seem to be hungry. And even when he does decide to eat, I'm sure I can get plenty of scraps from Kirsh, over in Kitchen Number Twelve."

Thrash lumbered over, carrying Airey's mug and a plate of fried salicornia and quorn nuggets. "Snack's on the house," growled Thrash. "Your pet's brought in extra trade tonight."

"Thank you, Thrash."

Klom picked up a nugget and held it under Tugger's nose. Sniffing without opening his eyes, Tugger made a polite refusal by lifting his paws to cover his face.

"See? He's not greedy or any trouble at all. Tugger only brings happiness and good luck."

Exasperated, Airey blew air rudely past his fluttering lips. "I give up. Sorrel, can you convince him to abandon this worthless foundling and get back to some fruitful exploration of – what did you say the ship's name was?"

"*Caution Discharge Zone.*"

"Hmm, a queer appellation. Well, Sorrel, go ahead. Lay your best arguments on our mighty yet stubborn friend."

Sorrel popped a nugget into her mouth. "Forget it, Airey. I'm sick of cajoling this idiot. It's like trying to teach a Tonshuan warthog to sing."

Airey pinched the corner of his mouth and rubbed a finger across his moustache. "Are we entirely certain this beast isn't valuable? After all, someone went to all the trouble of placing him in a suspensor-sac, however long ago. Klom, exactly what did our mighty overlord say when he inspected, ah, Tugger? And are you sure it was really him?"

Klom recalled.

At the foot of the ladder, Klom had exited the shaft and retrieved his sledge. He loaded Tugger onto it. The creature was alert, but still obviously weak and unsure from its long estivation. Klom had rested for a few minutes, refreshing himself with more water and cake, before setting out for the main port.

Out in the fresh air, Tugger visibly quickened. Rapaille, busy processing materials through the matter-modem, did not at first notice Klom and his living find. When he became aware of the rare discovery, Rapaille squawked with excitement and summoned one of his supervisors over his communicator. Harshly, the Quetzal pushed Klom aside and bent over Tugger.

"Please forgive the rude treatment you've received at the hands of this worthless drone, kindly sapient. You will soon be in touch with others of your kind, who will doubtless be overjoyed to know of your continued existence, and ready with a handsome reward."

In reply, Tugger laved Rapaille's face with his broad tongue.

"I don't think this one places so high on the sapient scale, Rapaille."

"Nonsense! Plainly an advanced being." Yet for all his blustering certainty, Rapaille regarded Tugger with a veneer of suspicion.

A personal lifter arrowed toward them in response to Rapaille's summoning. When it reached them, both Rapaille and Klom stared in disbelief.

The vessel held not a mere supervisor, but Bright Tide Rising himself. A sixstrand, the lanky Horseface was attended by a shimmering corona of majestatics that nearly concealed his head, yet he remained recognisable by his strangely articulated build and various family sigils worn as a gorget. Rapaille dropped to his knees and bowed. Klom remained standing.

Without consulting either Rapaille or Klom, Bright Tide Rising directed a portion of his swarm to engulf Tugger. After a swift examination, the units reunited with their peers. Pausing an unnaturally long time, the owner of the Asperna Yard finally delivered his verdict in a rumbling voice.

"Minimal sentience. Germline not on record. No talents, no adjuncts, no discernible worth. Dispose of the creature as you see fit."

As soon as Bright Tide Rising left, Rapaille berated Klom for twenty minutes for wasting the time of both himself and their ultimate patron. Klom absorbed the tirade placidly, then announced he was ending his shift early and returning to shore on the next transport. This news elicited further incoherent screeches from the Quetzal.

Now Klom repeated the Yard owner's assessment to Airey. The words seemed to deflate the slight, capricious fellow, but he soon regained his usual jovial air.

"Oh, well, there are months of salvage ahead. You'll hit the mother lode yet, Klom, I'm sure."

"Thank you, Airey."

The trio passed a few more hours drinking and chatting, eating and joking. Numerous individuals came over to examine Tugger. Klom felt proud.

At last, in the face of another workday, their beds beckoned.

Once outside, Sorrel stumbled in the near-lightless mucky path leading away from Thrash's, but Klom caught her before she could land in a patch of redolent luminous vomit, seething with intestinal symbionts. Tugger trotted along fastidiously behind. The dank air weighed like a blanket.

"Sorrel?"

"Uh, what –?"

"When did you ever taste Tancredi nectar?"

"One night, Jess – Jess Badura – he and me – you were sleeping –"

"Oh."

Sorrel stopped and hung with both hands from Klom's bicep. "You're not mad, are you, Klom?"

"No. I just like to learn things."

Three months into its disassembly, the *Caution Discharge Zone* appeared, from the outside, relatively unscathed. Here and there across its convoluted carcass new holes gaped, broken open to facilitate the removal of the ship's guts when the nearest port was inconveniently distant and a matter-modem could not be manoeuvred inside. Cormorants and kingfishers wheeled above the Vixen starliner, colonies roosting in selected niches and staining the slopes with their guano. A line of goose-barnacles had formed just below the high-water mark; at low tide, the exposed barnacles craned their mouthparts around on long necks, questing for the gnats that swarmed above the waters, the gnats in their turn attracted by the floating mats of seaweed that now trailed outward from the hull.

At a definite point in the near future, the *Caution Discharge Zone* would be reduced to an empty shell no taller than the line of barnacles, all its superstructure dismantled. At this point breakers skilled in underwater work would cut up the remaining shell and float the pieces away. The ship that had sailed the starwinds for an eon would be no more.

But right now, much still remained to be taken from inside.

Klom and Tugger arrived with the rest of their crew and marshalled outside the assigned entryway. Rapaille paid no notice to the oddball pair: a marked contrast to the first day Klom had shown up for work with his pet.

Fixing his hard eyes on Tugger, Rapaille had demanded, "Klom! What's the meaning of this pointless complication of your duties? Why is this worthless mass of protoplasm not already ground up into raw chuck for Kitchen Twelve?"

Klom did not exhibit any anger. But something in his voice made Rapaille flinch. "Tugger is my friend. No one hurts my friends."

Rapaille retreated. "All right then. But why not leave the beast in your crib?"

"There are too many bad people in the bustee. Someone might break into my crib and try to steal Tugger. Maybe even harm him. He doesn't know when people plan to do him harm. And he's too gentle to defend himself. I need to keep him by me all the time."

Realising when he was beaten, Rapaille angrily said, "Let the consequences of your soft-hearted stupidity be on your own head then! Tending to this monster will slow you down, and you'll soon be lying in a ditch with the Dungbeetles, begging paisa off the smart and sensible breakers who go about their work with vim and efficiency."

Klom made no reply, but simply marched inside the ship. Before they separated, Nyerephar and several other fellows congratulated him for standing up to Rapaille. Tugger came in for his share of the good will as well, accepting much petting and rib-thumping and shaking of his vestigal shoulder-hands.

Today, Klom and Tugger received no extra attention from anyone, so standard a part of the scene were they.

Half an hour's trudge through ravaged corridors and chambers, naves and apses, full of dangling cables and wires and sliced-open sheathing brought Klom and Tugger alone to the room where the breaker had left off work yesterday. The room was empty of furnishings, and only a scatter of devalued triptix littered the floor. The small personal data-palettes which had once carried routing instructions, dietary requirements, letters of introduction, shipboard credit-debit records, medical histories and other information needed by interstellar travellers now constituted nothing more significant than a drift of dead leaves.

One entire wall of this room presented a matrix of small doors inset with clear panels. Each door opened onto a long slim padded capsule plainly intended as a sleeping tube for members of some vaguely serpentine species. Each tube had to be disengaged from the matrix and stacked on the sledge. In one corner of the room squatted a large matter-modem. This deactivated cube, part of the intraship goods-transport system, presented no mirror face.

Klom fell to work, his head lamp casting all the illumination he needed. Tugger lay down peacefully on the hard floor and fell asleep. The puddle of drool spreading from his jowls caught glimmers from Klom's headlamp now and again.

In the three months Klom had owned his new pet, the man and beast had become inseparable, even off-duty. Sorrel had come to accept the new arrangement, grudgingly, while Airey simply disdained to pay any more attention to Tugger than he would have given to a familiar rug or table.

Several hours of hard work with spanner and snipper and prybar resulted in a sledge piled high with tubes. Klom must run these back to an active matter-modem before he could continue. But first he paused to refresh himself.

He took out his water bottle. Stretching sore muscles, he braced himself with his left hand against the dead matter-modem. He tilted back his head to glug a litre of warm musty liquid.

Ceiling lights flared improbably to life. So did the matter-modem.

Off-balance, Klom plunged in the mirror face up to his shoulder.

The lights snapped off. As did the matter-modem.

Klom howled. His arm had been sheared off clean at the shoulder. Vast quantities of blood sprayed the room. He fumbled frantically for a bungee, thinking to tie off his arteries. But there remained no flesh stub to bind.

Klom crashed to the floor like an uprooted Salembier sequoia. Consciousness slipped away from him like a school of fish from a disintegrating net.

"Tugger –"

Rapaille awaited the first of his crew to emerge with that day's salvage. He would key descriptions of the items into his reader, contributing to the vast inventory of parts being taken from the ship, then dispatch the parts through the matter-modem to the relevant disassembly stations and sorting lines. Meanwhile, he had nothing to do but wait and ponder the many injustices of his life. Standing in a shadow to escape the growing heat, he idly scanned the skies. A small Mlotmroz ship undoubtedly bearing buyers soared across his field of vision. Very good, the more customers the better for the Yard's business. All fortune to Bright Tide Rising! Rapaille's phantom wings itched, and he rubbed his wing stubs against the bulkhead. But the itching persisted. Life was unfair.

Someone burst crazily out of the port, jolting Rapaille out of his philosophical contemplation. That dumb man-ape, Klom, followed by his galloping worthless pet –

Klom bellowed. "Rapaille! Is there a crew mucking about with the ship's power generators?"

Rapaille boosted his haughty demeanor. "This is no business of yours! Get back to your wor – *urk*!"

Klom had gripped Rapaille's shirt with both his hands and lifted the avianoform off his feet, incidentally choking the

28

Quetzal with a knot of fabric at his throat. Klom thrust his face within centimetres of Rapaille and spoke with calm precision.

"You will call the crew working with the generators. You will tell them to be extra careful not to turn them on by accident. Or someone might get hurt. Do you understand?"

Rapaille understood that the person most likely to immediately get hurt was himself. So made a squawk he hoped Klom would interpret positively.

The huge breaker set his supervisor down and released him. After massaging his bruised throat, Rapaille placed the call Klom had ordered. Once Klom was satisfied, he turned away and climbed into a ship-to-shore barge, Tugger heeling behind his master.

"Take me back in," Klom told the bored Melungeon pilot.

As the barge pulled away, Rapaille sought to reassert his dignity and status. "Don't bother coming back for three weeks! Not till after Festival! You're on probation. Do you hear me, you addled eggsucker?"

But Klom never even looked back.

He seemed too busy stroking his left arm.

The long hot shed (its sides open for whatever chance breeze might arise) that housed Sorting Line Number Thirty-eight featured the following arrangement: ten parallel conveyor belts ran from one end of the shed to the other. The belts contributed a certain varying level of noise to the shed, depending on how dutifully a small army of oilers – mostly children – tended to them. At the head of each belt stood a matter-modem delivering the smaller pieces harvested from the ship under deconstruction. (Larger pieces not saved and sold as integral units went to disassembly stations first, then to the Sorting Lines.) Along both sides of each conveyor sat the sorters, staggered on three-legged stools at intervals of a metre or so. By the elbow of each sorter, mirror-face upwards, was a smaller matter-modem with a keypad that allowed a choice of destinations.

Each sorter had his or her or its special range of components to watch for. When spotted, the component would be snatched off the belt and dropped into the matter-modem. Simultaneous with the grab, the sorter would key in the relevant warehouse station to receive the transmission.

At the end of the belt waited a final matter-modem, to catch all the unclaimed pieces for further examination and categorisation.

The sorters were entitled to only as many lavatory breaks as minimally consistent with the most basic needs of their species. Lunches ran for half an hour, in shifts. Payment was based on speed and accuracy of performance, with debits taken for any missed pieces. So long as standards were maintained, conversation was permitted.

Sorrel was speaking to Aurinka, a Triffid who sat diagonally across from her. They were discussing jewellery. The Triffid waved several stalks decorated with hammered brass bracelets for Sorrel's admiration, while handling her duties competently with two other limbs.

Suddenly both Aurinka and Sorrel took notice of a distant commotion near one of the shed's entrances. They strained to ascertain what was going on without slackening production. The commotion seemed to be moving through the shed, getting closer to them. At last Sorrel saw the source of the upset.

Klom and Tugger bulled their way toward her, trailing protesting supervisors. When Klom spotted Sorrel, he bellowed out her name. Then he was upon her.

Grabbing Sorrel off her stool, Klom strongarmed her out of the shed, heedless of either her protests or her struggles to escape.

Once outside, Klom released her. They stood in the lee afforded by a mud-brick pissoir, while all around them surged unemployable or underage or offshift bustee-dwellers, a motley mass of scaled and chitinous, furred and slick-skinned beings, oblate or attenuated, faces like intricate masks or nearly featureless.

Sorrel faced Klom, full of fury. "You moron! What's the matter with you? I'm going to lose half a day's wages now!"

Klom's single-minded urgency seemed to evaporate. He faced Sorrel with a look that mixed contrition and confusion.

"Sorrel, I need your help. I died today."

This last sentence, delivered matter-of-factly yet with a detectable tremor, catalysed Sorrel's reaction from anger to a curious concern.

"What are you talking about? You're standing there as healthy as a Redskull ox."

"No, you don't understand. Here's what happened –" Klom recounted losing his arm in the matter-modem. "The last thing I remember is calling out for Tugger." The beast looked up at the sound of his name, offering a lopsided, slavering grin. "Then I blacked out. Not much time seemed to pass. Or maybe a lot. Anyway, I woke up whole."

Leerily, Sorrel regarded Tugger. "You're saying this creature was somehow responsible for regenerating your arm?"

"No, not exactly. You see, there was no blood anywhere any more. And my sledge was empty. I had filled it with tubes, but now it was empty. Then I looked at my reader, and it said the wrong time. I was in the past."

"That makes no sense at all."

Klom whirled savagely around and punched the wall of the lavatory, sending up a puff of mortar and pulverised soil. "I know, I know! But there's something else besides. Look at my skin!"

Sorrel examined Klom's outstretched hand, bloody-knuckled from impact with the wall. "Your cruft is gone!"

"All gone! That's right! But how?"

Sorrel shook her head in bewilderment. "I – I can't explain. Maybe Airey –"

"Airey! Of course! Let's go!"

Without waiting for her agreement, Klom hustled Sorrel away.

Tugger trotted blithely along behind them.

The fluids giving life to a typical starliner ranged from viscous hydrocarbon derivatives to thin plant-based extracts to exotically tinged protein-hormone-enzyme sera. These various liquids – some of which could be captured and sold, others of which went straight to crude disposal in the polluted swamps – invigorated a variety of mechanisms, all of which had to be drained before storage or disassembly. This task fell to the crews of the drainage pits.

Airey was right down in one of the pits, ankle deep in rainbow-sheened stenchy sludge. Unlike his downtime finery, his work uniform consisted of scarred boots and a patched brown coverall, its waterproofing peeling away in places. Employing a big spanner, he was struggling with the balky petcock of a suspended engine and cursing furiously.

"Motherless shit! Is this my reward for daring to aspire to elegance? May all the ancestors of all the mechanics who ever worked on this abomination freeze in the lowest levels of the Dimmig hells! Die, you bastard screwcap, die!"

Ranked at the edge of the pit, Airey's co-workers were enjoying his eloquent frustration. A Foraminifer was laughing so hard it kept dislocating its multiple jaws, resetting them each time with a grisly clacking of bone.

An instant cessation of the laughter caused Airey to crane his neck upward. Before he could react to the unexpected sight of Klom, he was lifted bodily from the pit.

"Come with me, Airey," Klom demanded. Airey caught Sorrel's eyes and read there the wisdom of complying. As the trio moved off for privacy, the drainman grabbed a rag to wipe his hands. Finished, he tucked it into a back pocket.

In the shadow of a belching, stinking cracking tower, Klom related his morning to Airey. Airey listened thoughtfully, his glance bouncing back and forth between Klom and Tugger. When Klom finished his account, Airey remained silent for half a minute before speaking.

"I see only one answer. Your pet can manipulate time in some fashion."

Klom's brow creased. "What? How could that be? I've never heard of such a thing being possible."

"Regardless of what we know, it's the only solution. Tugger responded to your distress by shuttling you back to the past. That explains your empty sledge and the timecheck on your reader."

"But how would that have fixed my arm? A dying time-traveller is still a dying man."

Airey stroked his negligible moustache. "This is true. The answer must be more complex then. I'll need to cogitate on this a while. But meanwhile, I think you should give Tugger anything he wants as a reward. Without him, apparently, you wouldn't be here right now. He's your guardian raksha."

"I'd gladly give him the finest meal or the thickest bed in the world. But all he seems to want is to be by my side!"

Airey hunkered down beside Tugger. He took the rag from his pocket and wiped away a line of saliva from Tugger's jowls. "There, there, good boy. What you want depends on what you are. And I guess we'll never know that. Unless –"

"Unless what?" asked Klom.

Airey straightened up, holding the rag bearing Tugger's drool before all their eyes as if it were a holy relic. "Let's send this sample to the laboratories at Radius Seven and get a genomic readout for Tugger. It will cost Klom a pretty paisa, but perhaps we'll learn more about our friend's constitution."

Sorrel said, "What could a simple lab analysis reveal that Bright Tide Rising and his majestatics overlooked?"

"I suspect that Tugger deliberately concealed his true nature from the Raisin, so that he would not be separated from Klom. Can we put anything beyond a being who can do what Tugger appears to have done for Klom?"

All three friends studied the innocuous animal with new respect. Tugger simply grinned dopily upward, then scratched behind his jaw with a rear paw, making a noise like a broom on sand.

Klom said, "Please see to it, Airey. We need to know what Tugger is so we can make sure he gets the proper treatment for his kind."

"Consider it done! And now, although *you* are suspended till after the Festival, Klom, Sorrel and I need to get back to work. Which brings me round to asking you for a small favour –"

Disdaining the spanner, Klom opened the stuck petcock with the force of his fingers alone. A torrent of purple, iron-smelling hematic coolant gouted out, splashing Klom to his knees, but he only laughed.

Klom's crib was luxurious by bustee standards. Scabbed together out of rusty sheet metal, driftwood posts and rafters, broad swaths of cured hides from Asperna's reptilian partchrumpfs and the odd bits of scratched plastic and warped pressboard, the shack leaked only minimally during the monsoon season and retained the heat from a seacoal fire well during the mild winters. Its interior held a hammock layered with rags and a teetering set of shelves hosting Klom's few possessions, including a photo of an old woman standing in front of a hut on a lakeshore. (The unframed photo was surrounded by deva medals distributed by the marabouts during various holy days, as if it were a small shrine.) A gamecube with a fuzzed-out display and half its functions deleted by age rested on a wicker hassock. Sorrel often

34

spent the night in Klom's crib, whether she and Klom had sex or not, preferring it to the crowded quarters she officially shared with a family of kitchen workers. The rancid oily smells her fellow tenants brought back in their clothing and hair from their shifts in the kitchen nauseated her.

This night, with Klom still unwontedly preoccupied by his earlier 'death', Sorrel elected to keep company with her lover after her shift ended. Their supper, taken amidst the crowded refectory attached to Kitchen Number Twelve, had been a silent affair.

They lay quietly together now in the hammock. The Great Sun had gone down just an hour ago, and, even without any exertion, their naked bodies – one sleek and golden, one hairy and pale – were bedewed with sweat. Estuarial breezes feathered their skins.

Strung from the two biggest, most solidly anchored posts, the hammock and its ropes nonetheless creaked as Sorrel shifted her position to clamber atop Klom. She began to kiss and tease him. "Where's the nasty old cruft then, sweetling? Nothing to stop me from rubbing my boobs here now, is there?"

Most unusually, Klom did not at first respond. Sorrel persisted however, and soon the shipbreaker began to react enthusiastically. One massive hand encompassed both her breasts, while the other cupped her whole ass. Straddling Klom's hips, Sorrel looked back over her shoulder to grab his penis and guide it home. But suddenly she stopped.

"Sorrel, what's wrong?"

"I – that thing is *watching* us!"

"What thing?" Klom raised himself up on one elbow. "Oh, Tugger?" The beast sat up on its back haunches attentively, legs askew toward one side and its bifurcate horn aimed straight at the couple. If interpreted anthropomorphically, its face expressed goofy bemusement. "But he's watched us every night since I found him."

35

"I know! But it's different now. We don't know what he is, or what he can do, or what he wants. It shivers my bones!"

"Tugger? Never! He's just my happy little friend. Like you and Airey."

Sorrel looked incensed, and she bounced off Klom to stand on the dirt floor. "So that's all I am to you? Some kind of pet? Where's my dress?"

Klom swung his legs around to sit upright. "No, Sorrel, you're not a pet. That's not what I meant to say. Don't twist my words around. You know I can't always say things just right. I love you. Come back, please."

Standing dressed by the plank door with a hand on the latchstring, Sorrel said, "Forget it, Klom. You seem to love this – this monster more than you do me. So why don't I just leave you two to whatever obscene pleasures you can contrive!"

Klom scowled. "Now, Sorrel, you know that's not –"

"And Airey deserves more respect from you too!" she yelled, then was gone.

Klom swore. He kicked his gamecube off the hassock and banged the door open. But Sorrel was already out of sight.

Tugger continued to beam beneficently, however, and eventually Klom calmed down. Before too long, both man and beast were snoring peacefully.

Klom's three weeks of probation were nearly over. He had spent the time increasingly frustrated by the realisation that the dismantling of the *Caution Discharge Zone* was proceeding swiftly without him. For one thing, he was losing taka and paisa every day he sat idle. His dreams of quitting the Yard and retiring to Chaulk seemed to recede further each day. To conserve his meagre savings – depleted drastically by the advance charges from the Radius Seven lab – Klom had taken to eating the very scraps from Kitchen Number Twelve which he had once foreseen as supplying Tugger's needs. (Luckily, that amiable companion continued, however improbably, to flourish on nothing more than air and water.) Soliciting the leftovers from the friendly but sardonic Bergamot cook named Kirsh was a chore that grew more odious to Klom each day. Kirsh's face, a pockmarked, damascene blue, would crack in a sarcastic snaggle-toothed smile as he handed over the leaky package of orts, always accompanied by some such jest as, "Here's fare fit for a fourstrand, Klom – a starving, poverty-stricken, imbecilic fourstrand, that is."

In truth, the loss of pay and the humiliating survival tactics represented the lesser of Klom's irritations. He found himself angrier over being excluded from the more intangible aspects of dismantling the starliner, the conversion of something useless into something useful. His earlier work on the ship had begun to foster an intimate bond with the vessel, an emotional linkage he had come to relish on previous jobs. And this particular bond had been sanctified in his blood (however inexplicably counterfactual that spillage had since become). It felt as if Klom had abandoned a responsibility to tend to the corpse of a loved one, leaving the job to strangers.

Few of these feelings were cast in words, either internally or to Sorrel or Airey. Nonetheless Klom experienced deep disquiet and irritability over this exclusion.

Each day he would spend hours on the shore, gazing out at the starliner, Tugger lying patiently in the sand at his master's feet. Tugger carried about a chewed hank of rope with him, and, from time to time, by obvious gestures, would try to interest Klom in a pulling game. Klom played with his pet once in a while, but more often Tugger was ignored, left to sleep or to fret at the frayed ends of the rope with his exiguous shoulder hands.

The mountainous ship just offshore exhibited few exterior changes, and Klom could only fantasise about the altered conditions of the interior. When the ship-to-shore ferry returned each night full of weary workers, Klom would be present at the dock to glower at Rapaille, who made certain to shelter himself amidst a knot of the brawniest breakers. But Klom never made a move on the overseer, knowing that the surest way to extend his probation would be another physical assault.

When Klom grew weary of staring out to sea, he retreated to one of the scrapheaps with his watercutter. There he would refine his already masterful carving skills by cutting up worthless old pods and wall fragments and contorted rebar with his illimitable tool, until the filthy dirt became a sea of mud. The fastidious Tugger chose to remain out of the way of the splattering, but always within easy hail.

It was at just such mindless pursuits that Sorrel found Klom this late afternoon.

"Klom! Are you mad? It's Festival Eve! The celebrations will start soon!"

The Festival of the Triple Sunset was an annual rite celebrating the conjoined westering of Great, Lesser and Least Suns. On the first night the three suns would set within several minutes of each other. On the final night the descent of the orbs would occur simultaneously, resulting in an incredible celestial display inspiring much reverence from the more devout citizens of the Yard and greater Asperna.

Klom holstered his watercutter. "I don't care about any stupid Festival."

"Oh, shut up and get over here. You've been moping for three weeks now, and enough is enough. You're going to have a good time tonight if I have to carry you on my shoulders!"

This ridiculous image amused Klom so much he laughed heartily for the first time in days. Squelching through the mud, he embraced Sorrel, causing her to squeal.

"You're filthy! Put me down!"

Klom complied. Tugger, excited, raced over and jumped up to lick Klom's face.

"Okay, let's go get drunk. Soon I'll be earning my wages again, so I'll treat tonight."

"Don't you want to change up first?"

"The hell with it. If I get drunk enough to fall down, my clothes will be dirty already."

The twilit, odoriferous streets and alleys of the bustee already swarmed with representatives of two dozen races. Chattering, clicking, cachinnating or cawing, the impoverished breakers and sorters, stockers and drainers, matter-modem techs and vegetable slicers all seemed determined to forget their cares and woes. Interspecies camaraderie reigned. Finery of a rudimentary sort had emerged from cheap chests and cardboard closets to adorn bodies spanning the spectrum from elongated to stubby, rugose to seamless, writhing to dignified.

Vendors with small braziers sold pungent kebabs of partchrumpf flesh. Bottles of liquor circulated freely from hand to tentacle to paw. Shadowy niches half-concealed the carnal explorations of chance-met lovers.

Klom moved through the exuberant chaos easily, the crowds parting before his mass. Sorrel and Tugger slipstreamed behind him. Klom gripped a half-empty flagon of toadchunder by its neck. A smear of partchrumpf grease ringed Sorrel's mouth. Tugger's tongue hung out.

At a cross-street, the crowd refused to give way for Klom and party, and he soon saw why. They had intersected a procession of marabouts and flagellants. Spinning their prayer wheels, swinging thuribles that wafted spicy fumes, the holybeings led an elaborately carved juggernaut pulled by a score of Sphinx. Hideous and benign wooden faces of devas gazed down implacably on the onlookers.

Sorrel shouted above the banging of drums, the keening of pandits, the crack of cattails threaded with bloody metal beads, and the blowing of horns. "Airey asked us to meet him later! He's got the results from Radius Seven!"

"Where?"

"He claims we need to keep the news secret. No eavesdroppers. So he said to meet at three AM by the stockpens. No one will be in such an unlikely place at that hour."

By two-thirty in the morning, Sorrel was growing weary. Klom's vigour, unfettered from any brooding, ran unabated. Tugger dragged along gamely.

"Let's find Airey so we can get to bed, Klom."

"All right."

The stockpens housed various softly lowing food beasts for the kitchens, behind shimmering, sizzling lines of force running from stanchion to stanchion. The noisome atmosphere insured that celebrants avoided the acreage.

"Airey!" yelled Klom semi-drunkenly into the luminance-crosshatched blackness. "Here we are! Show yourself, man! Or are you too busy sucking the ten teats of a Milchmaid!"

Airey stepped from the shadows, hissing. "Quiet, you big 'rumpf! Do you want every bravo in the vicinity to come investigate your bellowings? I saw a pair of Grimjacks just a few alleys over! We're here to discuss something extremely vital."

Klom sobered up. "What have you learned about Tugger? What makes him so important?"

Airey flourished a data-palette, while Sorrel gripped Klom's arm and leaned in closer. "Your foundling is a *twelvestrand*, Klom! An incredibly powerful deva, despite his seeming lack of sapience! Perhaps the only one of his kind. But unlike all other devas, he's metastable on our ontological plane! And he might very well be the Book of Forgetting as well!"

"The Book of Forgetting? But –"

Airey gestured dismissively. "I know, I know, everyone has assumed for millennia that the Book was an artifact of some sort. But I've been doing research into the legend, and nothing in the fragments of lore is really inconsistent with the Book being a living creature. After a little cogitation, I realised how your pet saved your life. He doesn't travel *back* in time, but *crosswise*! He forgets one universe while remembering another. And somehow he shunted the essence of your consciousness onto an alternate timetrack along with him. A timetrack that lagged just a little beyond our moment, where your accident never happened. If you wish to quibble, this universe is not the one you were born in."

The hesitant tone of Klom's speech conveyed a slowly dawning understanding. "But then, that means – I guess Tugger is really valuable." Klom looked down at his pet. The being whose inherently recomplicated cellular structure allowed him to transcend limitations of space and time and leap across the multiverse was busy nibbling at his own hide for pests.

Airey laughed cynically. "That's understating the case a million times worse than a Neftali trader misrepresents his wares! With Tugger by your side, you can lay claim to all the riches in the Indrajal."

"I don't want so much, though," said Klom. He gathered his friends to his side. "Just enough for the four of us to leave this hard place and retire to Chaulk –"

The next voice, a basso rumble, shocked them all, although only Klom recognised it. "I am afraid no one is going anywhere."

Bright Tide Rising floated above them, clouded by his majestatics. The sixstrand owner of the Asperna Yards stayed silent for a long moment – possibly regarding the quartet curiously through his mutable veil, although Klom could not say for sure – before speaking at last.

"A metastable creature with twice my own information density. No wonder I was unable to read it properly. It is hard to credit such a miracle, although I have never known the scientists at Radius Seven to be mistaken before. You will now give me that data-palette."

Airey braced his spine. "Klom paid for these tests, so they belong to him. And so does Tugger."

"Absolutely incorrect. The creature is salvage from a ship owned by me. It is mine by terms of your employment. Your co-worker will be compensated for his find. Perhaps I will give him as much as ten thousand taka."

Sorrel chimed in. "That's an insult! This animal is invaluable!"

"And you three are all too stupid and primitive to properly exploit such a treasure. But I am done arguing. With the creature's entire genome on a palette, it will be simple to rebirth him, this time without any misplaced allegiances. I have no further need of any of you."

Klom felt mentally yanked in a dozen different directions. How had this horrible situation come about, from such simple and innocent impulses? But before he could speak or act, the telecosmic corona of majestatics around Bright Tide Rising seemed to squirt four solid streams of particles, distributed along four vectors.

Klom's watercutter practically leaped into his right hand, even as he hurled himself to one side. He felt a piercing pain in his left shoulder. But the pain did not disturb his aim.

The noise that Bright Tide Rising's legs made in falling to the ground was followed in milliseconds by the accompanying mucky splash of his separate upper half.

Klom turned to his companions. All three were stretched out unmoving on the filthy ground. One by one, he searched their corpses for wounds. But the lancelike majestatics had pierced so cleanly, yet so fatally, that Klom could detect nothing. At least their deaths had been swift. There was very little blood, and in fact his own shoulder wound was invisible and unleaking.

Klom lifted first Sorrel's head from the muck, and kissed her dirty cheek. He did the same for Tugger and Airey, before turning to their killer.

Bright Tide Rising's myrmidons were attempting to put their master back together. They had already gathered up his spilled entrails and dragged his two halves into contact and were stitching golden sutures inside and out.

Klom carved the sixstrand into pieces so small that all the majestics in the Indrajal would not suffice to repair the Horseface. Then he kicked shitty, hay-speckled mud atop the carrion.

The long, harsh night was waning, with dawn a distant rumour. Klom stood, half-bewildered, in his twilit shack. In his hand he held the data-palette bearing Tugger's genome. What good was it to him? The sum required to reincarnate Tugger was far beyond his means. And even if somehow miraculously given the fee, Klom could engineer the conception only of Tugger's mere doppelganger, a blank slate with no familiar consciousness shared with the original who had saved Klom's life.

And now he was in danger of losing his own life once more. His murder of Bright Tide Rising, even in self-defence, would earn him death, under the laws of the Indrajal, which were biased against twostrands.

He knew that he must run. But where?

Klom gathered up a couple of possessions: the picture of his mother, a few deva medals handed out at religious ceremonies. But then he was overwhelmed by fatigue and despair. The lack of a certain destination left him feeling hopeless. With near-suicidal unselfconcern, he dropped into his hammock and fell asleep among his rags.

Sometime in the earliest hours of morning he awoke to a wet tongue rasping his face. He flailed his arms about, confused and slow to emerge from dreams, and encountered a familiar boulder of a head bearing a fleshy protuberance.

"Tugger?"

Something hard was spat out onto his chest, bouncing off into the hammock.

By the time Klom got his eyes ungummed and open, he was alone again.

A data-palette slimed with saliva shared the hammock with him. He dried it off on his shirt and jacked it into his reader.

The palette was a triptix in Klom's name. It registered a spendable value above the ticket price of several million taka, and listed as the bearer's ultimate destination the fabled world of Mount Sumeru.

Klom gazed around him at the familiar shabby interior of his crib.

Already it looked distant and remote. The picture of his mother on the banks of Lake Zawinul seemed to represent a stranger. Klom sensed wordlessly that he would never return to Chaulk.

Many questions and a sense of mystery suffused him. Was Tugger somehow alive? What awaited him on Mount Sumeru?

Only travel out among the worlds of the Indrajal held hope of answers.

Two

Worldshifter

"I dropped off into a restless dream about a big room full of noise and excited faces, and a smaller room with smoke curling out past an open door, and a big tank, painted green. There was a man in a white uniform with blood on his face, and a woman, crying, and I was saying, "That's an order, damn your guts!" And then they were all backing away and I picked up the bundle in my arms and went in through the smoky door and heard behind me the sound of the woman, crying..."

— *The Day Before Forever*, Keith Laumer

Waiting nervously at the gate to the starquay, Klom irritably tugged at the hem of a tight sleeve ringing his massive upper arm. His new clothes troubled him. Used to going mostly naked or raggedly clad in the semitropical climate of Asperna, he found that wearing even a snugglet was irksome. This clinging smart singlet suit in pleasingly organic patterns of taupe and ochre covered him from mid-thigh up to neck and down to biceps, leaving the rest of him bare, save for a pair of adaptive minimus peds. Klom felt the gentle enwrapment of the suit to be a constriction and a hindrance, a reminder of some heretofore hidden obligation or duty to society that he had previously managed to shirk. In truth, his range of motions was as utterly free as it had ever been while he was wresting, bare-chested, some

45

balky component from its housing on board a derelict starship. But the symbolism of his new attire – a metaphysical concept Klom struggled to fully formulate – conveyed only a cumbersome snaffling of his authentic nature.

But, unfortunately, he had to be conventionally clothed upon venturing into the greater galactic milieu, the Indrajal.

Should he even be so fortunate as to escape the planet after his murder of Bright Tide Rising.

When the light of day had begun to seep through the seams of his crib, Klom performed his rude ablutions. His shoulder throbbed and ached where it had been pierced, but seemed relatively uninflamed, despite the dirt of his surroundings. Such was the lucky result of the nearly surgical drilling by the deadly majestatics. He had sustained worse wounds on the job. Klom resolved to attend to it at some point.

Small quantities of dried blood from his inspection of the corpses of his three friends still flecked his skin. How could the lovely Sorrel, the whimsical Airey and the loyal Tugger possibly be dead? And if the last-named had indeed perished, despite possessing a kind of mighty power in his hypothetical role as the Book of Forgetting, who or what had visited Klom in the dark?

Such irresolvable thoughts swirled confusingly through Klom's brain – but not to such a distracting extent that he failed to focus on his escape.

The majestatics attendant on Bright Tide Rising had surely recorded Klom's crime. But here was the one element of grace: who could they report to?

Bright Tide Rising was the sole sixstrand on the planet, Asperna being his personal dominion. There was no higher authority here to receive the news of the murder and come after Klom. Lieutenants, trained to be subservient, would never take the initiative to bring their master's killer to account. And interstellar communication happened only as fast as ships bearing messages could travel – a matter of days or weeks. So if Klom could leave the planet before a response could be mounted, he might yet elude any unfair justice.

Although what risks he would face out in the Indrajal as a fugitive, he could not imagine.

First things first: a visit to the mercantile that serviced this district of the sprawling bustee.

The place was run by a Fleerowl named Alula. Highly devout, the aged avianoform kept her shelves full of animated celestial icons, portraits of famous marabouts, and touchstones that broadcast mental sensations that faintly recalled what it felt like to be in a deva's presence.

Luckily, at such an early hour there were no other customers present to wonder about Klom's sudden need for fancy new garments.

"Alula, I need some respectable clothes. But I don't want to look flashy."

Alula proffered a reader. "Have a glim at the catalogue."

Klom picked out a simple intelligent suit. Alula nodded approval. "A very good choice. But of course, I don't have your size handy. So big! No matter. I'll get it via modem."

Within half a minute, Klom's suit had been delivered through the mirror face of the mercantile's portal device. He also selected a handsome shoulder-strap satchel made of Salembier grunter leather, paid for both – from his labourer's account, not daring yet to use the mysterious data-palette bestowed on him by being or beings unknown just a few hours ago – donated a few taka to the shrine on the counter, causing its crystals to shimmer anew and eliciting a beaky grin from Alula, and then hastened to his crib.

How long did he have before Bright Tide Rising's vengeful peers came after him? And, assuming he escaped: where was he headed, and what was his mission?

Both questions he put off until such time when he could feel safer.

Now, awaiting entrance to the busy industrial port where the heterogenous repurposed industrial cargo from Asperna was sent starwards, Klom felt the hot breath of pursuit on his neck, although no actual authorities had yet manifested.

Without cause or interest during his uncomplicated past, Klom had never visited the starquay before. Situated several kilometres beyond the shabby margins of the shantytown, the palisaded conglomeration of warehouses and extensive service pads for the arrival and departure of the wavepacket vehicles that circulated among the worlds of the Indrajal, represented to Klom the gateway to an almost unimaginable realm. The shushed fall and rise of the ships, the scurrying of the ground crews and labourers and officials, the rapid crisscrossing of ground vehicles, wheeled and floaters, everyone wallowing under the heat of all three lofty suns, induced a kind of nervous vertigo in the giant. But then an image of Tugger, and the memory of his companion's unflappable calm, rose to steady him.

Now the line of travellers – a dozen assorted sapients of some distinction and privilege, all with legitimate business concerns, no one else a fugitive shipbreaker – began to advance. Klom shuffled forward.

The official at the gate was a fellow human, a light-skinned fellow with sandy hair, wearing what looked to be a very uncomfortable uniform for this world's climate: long sleeves and trousers patterned with corporate sigils.

When Klom drew abreast of the man, he tendered the data-palette that had been so strangely dropped into his lap.

The gatekeeper slotted it into a reader, studied the display. His eyes widened.

"This identifies you as Klom of Chaulk, a shipbreaker of indigo stripe."

"Yes." Klom awaited pronouncement of his arrest. He fantasized about briefly overpowering the official, somehow dashing onto a ship just about to depart, stowing away –

"But your documents also state that Klom of Chaulk is just a secondary identity, strictly temporary, to facilitate confidential market research. Your primary Indrajal ID is that of Brum Bravalo, flavour-water magnate from Demigrieve. You are booked all the way through several nexial transitions to – Mount Sumeru? Is this correct?"

Stunned, Klom hesitated only a moment. "Yes, of course."

"Very well, *Khun* Bravalo. All is in order. Your passage aboard the *Squall of Demons* is confirmed. Pad thirty-nine, departure in one hour."

A bevy of majestatics swarmed Klom as soon as he stepped aboard the *Squall of Demons,* and he came to a dead halt in dread. Were these killer drones, sent to enforce a mortal sentence upon him? But when they clustered only around his wounded shoulder, obviously intent on repairing it, Klom relaxed.

As fellow passengers detoured around Klom, a porter appeared at Klom's side in the spacious entryway of the ship, a short and rotund sapient of a species unknown to Klom. The being resembled one of the cheerful bristly burrowing creatures Klom knew from the forest around his native Lake Zawinul. Thoughts of the childhood refuge recalled the portrait of his mother in his satchel. Would he ever see her again in this lifetime? Klom had his doubts. Probably he was embarked on a one-way fool's errand. If only he could have taken the newfound wealth on his data-palette (was it Brum Bravalo's purloined hard-earned life savings, if such a person even existed?) and simply retired on Asperna. But his murder of the sixstrand overlord had precluded that.

The little steward piped up. "The name is Lingle, *Khun* Bravalo, here to assist you during your trip. The reparative treatment on your injury is courtesy of Retta Galaxyliners, as we assess your health to ensure fellow passengers against any communicable diseases. 'Your carnal cares constitute our happy *giri.*' Have you no other luggage?"

Finished knitting up and disinfecting Klom's wound, the microworkers flew away. Klom flexed the joint and was grateful to feel nearly normal again. "No, just this satchel."

"Allow me then. I will guide you to your cabin."

Klom had the strangest sensation as Lingle conducted him through the corridors and levels of the ship. After taking apart so many obsolete and discarded starcraft, all antiques, Klom felt as if this still-functioning vessel was not a contemporary artifact, but rather some ghost from the past, and he himself a time-traveling phantom, hurled backwards to another era. The reality of current-day star travel had not really registered on him while he still laboured in the Shipbreakers' Yard. Stargoing vessels were always only ancient dead things.

The *Squall of Demons* was not very large – certainly no mountain such as the *Caution Discharge Zone* where he had found Tugger. Klom guessed it might hold one hundred passengers, and seemed not even full today. After all, what could bring outsiders to Asperna other than commercial goals? The planet, so far as Klom knew, was no tourist destination, no centre of culture, no political powerhouse. Its sole industry was shipbreaking, and these departing travellers must have all been conducting business of one kind or another with Bright Tide Rising's enterprises.

Klom wondered if they knew yet that the sixstrand was dead. And if they had heard the news, could they ever imagine that the killer resided among them?

Klom's cabin proved to be much bigger than his entire old crib. Softly glowing light panels, cushy bed, decorative artwork on the walls. Not the height of luxury, he was sure, but still more lush and pampering than any environment he had ever found himself in before.

"How many must I share this room with?"

Lingle showed professional unflappability. "A fine jest, *Khun* Bravalo. You are the sole occupant of this suite."

The porter demonstrated all the facilities, and then waited obsequiously by the door. Klom hesitated as to what was required of him, then spontaneously recalled tossing coins into a jar for the bartender at Thrash's shabeen. He sent Lingle a few taka via the ether, and the response from the hedgehog-man indicated Klom had done the right thing.

"You will find the hours for dining listed in the online directory, and of course you may have any meals brought directly to your room."

"Is this vessel going nonstop to Mount Sumeru?"

"Again, *Khun* Bravalo expresses his wit. This is only the regular shuttle between Asperna and Onza-Gora. You must change starliners there for any subsequent destinations."

Alone in his sumptuous quarters, Klom stripped off his confining singlet suit and luxuriated in his freedom. He took a long shower, marvelling at the seemingly endless hot water and fragrant soaps. How Sorrel would have loved this! Why had her life been cut so short? What evil had she ever done to merit such a sad end? Associating with Klom was her only crime. And Klom's loving possession of Tugger had been that companion's only transgression. The world was unfair and brutal. People died for no reason. If only –

Klom sat down at the desk hosting the cabin's reader. He slotted in the data-palette that verified his assumed identity and wealth, and which charted his intinerary to Mount Sumeru, far across the galaxy. What awaited him there?

He popped out that particular mysterious ultrafiche and inserted the other one he carried, obtained through Airey: the transcription of Tugger's genome. The long recomplicated scroll of twelvestrand genetic coding conveyed nothing of course to Klom's uneducated eyes, until an app in the reader produced a visualisation of the genome's somatic instructions, plus-or-minus percentages of accuracy flickering alongside the image.

There on the screen showed the familiar friendly quadruped beast whom Klom had rescued from the suspensor-sac: the boulder-headed, stubby-legged, barrel-bodied, antenna-graced creature who supposedly represented a power beyond any other in the universe.

But all Klom saw was someone who loved him, had saved his life, and whom he had loved in return.

The fifth port of call after leaving Asperna – still not a quarter of the way to Mount Sumeru – was a world named Stratcom, the oldest, most cultured, most complex, and most densely populated planet encountered so far on Klom's odd and incalculable journey through the Indrajal.

Faced with the noisy swarming warren of streets in the city of Sedge that hosted the enormous starquay where his ship had just landed, Klom felt at first utterly baffled. How to hail transportation, where to find lodgings, what kind of food was suitable for humans, how to go about locating an expert strandcrafter who could bring Tugger – or his DNA cousin – back to life. These matters and more fell beyond even his new competence gained after three weeks of travel. A changed man from the simple labourer from Lake Zawinul, Klom nonetheless remained basically what he had always been: a slow-thinking, deliberate, straightforward plodder.

Thank the devas, then, for the presence of Lingle.

That small, spiny-pelted, portly bundle of energy and efficiency had already summoned a hired car with enough storage capacity to hold the two large floater trunks that carried the belongings of the pair. Lingle's wordly goods from his years of stewardship aboard various Retta Galaxyliners had been hosted in one trunk aboard the *Squall of Demons*, while Klom's new purchases from his prior planetary stops had required the second luggage.

"You simply must have more and better clothes, *Khun* Bravalo. You can't wear that, ah, utilitarian garb under all polite circumstances. Most offputting and déclassé, I am sure. No matter how deeply you 'went native' during your investigations on Asperna, you absolutely must reengage with society on society's terms, now that you are back among your peers."

"If you say so, Ling, for you always know best."

The trip from Klom's homeworld of Asperna to Onza-Gora had taken five days. During the entire first day of the voyage, Klom had been reluctant to leave his cabin, for fear of doing something that would get him in trouble. Although what mere social infraction he could incur that would be worse than murdering a sixstrand, he could not imagine.

Paying him frequent visits during that first day to ascertain and fulfil his needs, Lingle had proven to be an essential aide, confidante, and reliable source of information. None of Klom's questions, however unsophisticated, had been met with disdain. Instead, the little Vib – the homeworld of his kind, Vibbsy, had been incinerated during a commercial war some centuries ago, leaving the scattered survivors of the species as stateless workers – showed a professional compassion and deference to the naïve Klom; an attitude which, Klom sensed, was not derived wholly from receipt of wages and tips, but also somewhat based on a native affability and empathy.

Eventually, reassured by Lingle's gentle guidance, Klom had ventured out to the various lounges, spas, gamerooms and refectories aboard the galaxyliner, and even found himself making rudimentary conversation with his fellow passengers. As he had suspected, they were assorted business types, and seemed most interested in hearing details of Klom's own beverage enterprises, his profession having been made public on the ship's virtual roster. Klom managed to fabricate some vague details that seemed to satisfy his interlocutors, who, truth be told, wanted mainly to talk about themselves. A couple of women and one man seemed interested in Klom as a bed partner, but he turned them all down, the memories of Sorrel still too painful.

Even these limited interactions and dialogues led Klom to one conclusion: the Indrajal was a complex, bewildering place, and if he were to have any success in his quest he would need to enlist some help. By the time the ship was one day away from Onza-Gora, Klom had made up his mind about what to do.

Busy with preparations for arrival, Lingle found time to respond to Klom's call. He entered Klom's cabin with his usual professional deference. "Your summons, *Khun* Bravalo, failed to make explicit your needs."

"Sit down, will you, Lingle. I want to talk with you."

The Vib took a seat sized for Klom, a perch that left his feet dangling in mid-air.

Klom felt nervous. "Have a drink. This stuff is very smooth. Never had anything like it at Thrash's shabeen."

"Zoycean Green Mist? Smooth indeed. I will indulge in only a thimblesworth, and strictly pursuant to your command."

The liquor relaxed both Klom and the steward.

"Lingle, I want to share with you my true background."

"As you wish."

Klom disclosed his real history and recounted everything that had led to his departure from Asperna. Lingle listened with seeming imperturbability. Nonetheless, midway through the recitation the Vib felt compelled to help himself to a second, much larger drink.

Upon concluding his tale, Klom said, "So you see, Lingle, I have a long and strange road ahead of me, and I need a loyal, smart and capable companion. I think that's you. Would you ever agree to help me in my quest?"

Lingle pushed meditatively at one corner of his mouth with a forefinger that hosted a thick black clawlike nail. "You are asking me to throw over my steady and reliable employment of two decades standing, all to accompany a wanted criminal across the galaxy in search of a will-o-the-wisp?"

"I guess so. But I can pay you good. What do you make now as a steward?"

"Ten thousand taka per annum."

"I'll pay you ten times that."

"Generous indeed. But mere money is not a sufficient inducement. Tell me again about this being you named Tugger."

"Here, have a look at him." Klom caused the reader to display Tugger's conjectured portrait drawn from the genome record.

Lingle studied the image. "An unprepossessing countenance. And yet you dare to make the claim that this entity is synonymous with the Book of Forgetting? The annunciation of that being is said to herald a revolution among all the strata of the Indrajal, from devas on down. A recalibration of all relationships and values."

"Lingle, listen real close to me now. All that is beyond me. It might be true, it might not. I don't make any claims, because I don't know anything about anything. Except that I miss Tugger and want him back. That's my whole notion."

Lingle said nothing for a minute, then spoke a seeming non-sequitur. "Do you know how and why Vibbsy was destroyed?"

"No, of course not. I never heard of your birth planet till I met you. But I sure am sorry you lost your world."

"I appreciate your sympathy. The manner of its demise was such. Two sixstrands – Accidental Beauty and Damascene Indigo Feather – both wanted a monopoly on my homeworld's strangelet mines. They could not come to terms, and were too equally balanced in their powers to achieve a victory by force. So they both decided that rather than let a rival win, they would destroy the planet. Accidental Beauty planted a hardened, stellar-rated matter modem at the very centre of the planet and opened it up to a hundred receivers that gushed live magma onto the

55

surface of Vibbsy. Not to be outdone, Damascene Indigo Feather triggered a critical mass of strangelets into a planetary cascade of matter transmutation. My species had a choice between incineration and molecular decoherence."

Klom stayed silent for a spell, then said, "I guess my homeworld got off easy, then. All we had to endure under the rule of Bright Tide Rising was poverty, maiming, and dying young."

"Indeed. So as you might surmise, I harbour no love for the terabase elite who run roughshod over the galaxy. If your quadruped Book of Forgetting could bring some rebalancing of the scales of justice to the Indrajal –"

"I can't guarantee that, Lingle."

The Vib considered the situation while gnawing on a nail, then leaped from the chair. "Damn all certainty! I've spent too long in a rut of false security! I'm throwing in with you, *Khun Bravalo*, mad as you may be!"

"That is wonderful! But please, call me Klom. That's my real name."

Lingle considered. "No, I think not. Best for you to go by your assumed identity. Especially if any of the terabases are still vigilant for your reappearance."

"I never thought of that! See, your wisdom is paying off already, Ling!"

"Time will tell."

Tendering his resignation at the offices of Retta Galaxyliners on Onza-Gora (the wavepacket stewards had no long-term contract with their employers, but worked strictly on the sufferance of the corporation and subject to their own whims), Lingle announced his intention to outfit his new boss more appropriately. But first, another mission, accomplished right at the same offices but at the transit counter: to purchase tickets for Lingle matching Klom's mystery itinerary.

When finished, Lingle studied their route silently for a time, then said, "Mount Sumeru. I never fancied I would visit that wondrous impossible place."

With any other being, Klom might have hesitated to reveal his ignorance. But already he felt fully at ease with Lingle. He had a strong intuition that only ultimate honesty between them would serve them best and promote their survival and success.

"What is Mount Sumeru, Ling? Why is it so special?"

"It is a solar system featuring one million habitable planets, that's all."

Klom pondered. "A solar system. That's one sun and all its worlds, right?"

"Concisely stated and generally accurate, but not exhaustively definitive."

"How can one sun be the mother to a million worlds?"

"Mount Sumeru is an array of three dozen suns, held in place by a supermassive black hole at the centre of the matrix."

"Those words confuse me. I can't picture such a thing."

"In that you are not alone. I understand that only seeing the astronomical construction up close can even partially convey the magnitude of its reality."

"I guess I'll just have to wait then."

"As will I."

A more practical consideration popped up in Klom's mind. "If there's a million planets at Mount Sumeru, which one is our destination?"

"An excellent question, *Khun* Bravalo! Our ticket only specifies arrival at one of the many distal receiving stations that serve as gateways for out-system visitors."

"Guess it'll all work out somehow."

"Your naïve faith is infectious! Although like all infections, it requires close monitoring. Now, let's get you some decent clothes!"

After that, the pair found nothing to do but follow the pre-planned intersystem itinerary that the enigmatically bestowed ultrafiche had laid out for them. Khush, Dustbowl, and Badura were pleasant but unexceptional worlds, mere stepping stones holding no obvious answers to Klom's quest, and their prearranged bookings had the travellers leaving almost as soon as they arrived. They used the transit time to become better acquainted with each other, to make nebulous plans for the future, and to foster Klom's education.

Quizzing the big shipbreaker, Lingle found him lamentably deficient in common knowledge of the Indrajal – although he did have praise for Klom's 'alley smarts'. And so the little Vib commenced to tutor the man in the basics that would aid him to move without too many hindrances through the Indrajal.

Lingle maintained a non-supercilious, professorial attitude, never commenting on any amazing gap, however rudimentary, in Klom's worldview. He seemed genuinely interested in expanding Klom's horizons and dispelling his uncertainties, and for this Klom was grateful. Only once did Lingle let loose an impulsive chittering laugh.

"Tell me again," said the Vib, "exactly how you discovered your friend Tugger in his stasis pod."

"Well, it happened when we were assigned to decommission a ship named the *Caution Discharge Zone* –"

Lingle's explosive amusement could not be contained. When the little factotum finally assumed a sober look, Klom asked what had been so funny, and Lingle explained.

"You mistook a familiar warning placard for the ship's name."

Klom felt then the immense weight of his ignorance. He began to say that he had merely accepted the misinformation that his coworker Nyerephar had blithely offered. But he stopped short, acknowledging to himself that he had always before now walked through his own life with a kind of lazy acceptance of hearsay and the opinions and choices of others, rather than exert his own intelligence, however slight when compared to the norm of his fellows. But such slackness could no longer suffice. Not in a universe where all hands were raised, if not in opposition to him, then in a negligent dismissal of his worth and needs.

His feelings unhurt, Klom grinned broadly. "That was kind of dumb, wasn't it?"

"Dumb, my dear student, is a relative, improvable condition which only becomes contemptible when it is cherished."

"If you say so, Ling."

By the time the unlikely pair disembarked at Sedge on Stratcom, Klom felt very much smarter than the brutish fellow who had been content to chop up ancient starliners all his life. But to his surprise, he discovered that he did not derive a sense of security or pride from his learning, but only a larger sense of how much remained outside his ken.

Within twenty minutes of their landing, Lingle had selected for them a tolerable inexpensive hotel in a slightly louche neighbourhood, run by a family of fastidious, naturally talcum-scented Pinemartens, the smallest of whom resembled a ball of fur propelled by a perpetual-motion engine.

Up in their room, Lingle said, "I know you have several million taka on your fiche, but there is no telling what expenses we shall incur on this wild nildoror chase. So best to economise now. Hence our less-than-plush accommodation."

"This place is still fancier than I'm used to, Ling. It's good. Say, maybe I should check our credit balance. We did spend some extra on Badura."

"Only because you had to recompense that café owner for damages incurred to his establishment."

"But he called you a slimy water rat!"

Lingle sighed. "As a planetarily orphaned species, I am used to such slurs. Did you hear me take offense?"

"No... So that's why I had to do it for you!"

Klom slotted his palette into the portable reader that Lingle carried. He stared at the screen, then turned the reader toward Lingle. Instead of credit balance, a name, title and address showed, unprompted.

Nomar Zabumba
Expert Strandcrafter
Morgay Prospect
District of the Wells

"What does it mean, Ling?"

"It seems we are being directed towards a meeting by whoever gave you this fiche. But I swear the palette is not ensouled, and we have no outside connections on this reader. So how this new information is being planted, I cannot say."

Klom leaped up from his seat on the edge of the bed and grabbed his companion's hand. "Who cares? We have a destination, so what're we waiting for! Let's go!"

Lingle's feet never touched another surface until they were ensconced in a tuk-tuk whose driver nodded in easy recognition at the address they provided.

Whatever the ancient origin of its name, the District of Wells proved deficient in springs, fountains or watering holes, comprising several urban blocks indistinguishable from the others they had passed through: an assortment of heterogeneous extruded grown and self-assembled buildings hosting retailers, food stands, small fabs and upper-story apartments. Walls crawled with animated signage. Children racketed from a null-gee playground. The smell of some kind of fried fish vied with perfume odours spilling out of salons where fur, hair, feather, chitin and scales all received equal grooming attentions. The sidewalks hosted a plethora of different races.

The façade of Nomar Zabumba's establishment featured many screens displaying his accomplishments: cherished progeny tailored to the minutest specifications; chimeric pets assembled from impossible combinations both horrific and kawaii; industrial hybrids hard at work, digging, lifting, transporting.

Klom devoted little attention to the displays, but instead hustled through the door, followed by a scampering Lingle, hard-pressed to keep up.

The interior was a pleasantly lighted and discreet showroom with a service counter. Various small models of assorted biological creations, plus some flat static images of vats, wombs and alembics. Some multivalent seating arrangements.

Before Klom could holler out for assistance, a door at the rear of the store opened, and out skittered a midsized being who presumably must be Nomar Zabumba

The proprietor was a Pryle. His body resembled a giant russet cereal biscuit, all thatched fibres. Parallel rows of finger-like feet on his underside offered potentially omnidirectional progress. Four tendril-like arms, ending in subtle manipulators, emerged symmetrically from the body. The Pryle's head – a globe with a ring of eyes around the equator, an iris-like mouth, and no nose – rested atop a corkscrew neck now coiled, mid-upper-body, into a supportive pile like some dockside heap of rope.

"Do you know me?" demanded Klom.

The Pryle's voice sounded rather gelatinous. "Why no, good *Khun*. Should I?"

"We were directed to you."

"By whom?"

Klom was stumped. Lingle stepped forward. "*Khun* Zabumba, I believe we have something of interest to show you. *Khun* Bravalo, please tender the genome fiche to our savant."

Klom handed over the palette containing Tugger's specs. Zabumba slotted it and studied the output for a considerable time in silence. His ring of eyes blinked in sequence several times, and his neck uncurled so that his head could bob up and down in a kind of shrug og astonishment. Finished, he reluctantly handed the fiche back.

"A genuine twelvestrand. I never thought to see such a thing. I thank you for bringing this to me. May I ask his provenance?"

Klom gave a condensed version of Tugger's life and death, omitting all of Klom's own crimes and the possibility that Tugger was the legendary Book of Forgetting. "Can you recreate him?"

"It would take every iota of skill I possess. But it would be the capstone of my career. I can but try."

"And your fee?" inquired Lingle.

"I should perhaps pay you for the privilege. But I cannot afford the commensurate amount. And my time and prowess, not to mention the cost of raw materials and reactor hours, are not negligible – let us say, three-quarters of a million taka."

"Half that sum."

"Come now! The crafting the mitochondria alone will take me dozens of hours!"

"All right then, four hundred thousand."

"You jest with me!"

After further bargaining, a price of six-hundred-and-twenty-five thousand was agreed upon. Klom reluctantly handed over the irreplaceable genome fiche, made a partial downpayment, settled on an estimated date of delivery, then left the shop.

"I told you we had to conserve our funds, *Khun* Bravalo, and now you see why. Expenditures known and unknown lie ahead. Still, saving us a hundred-and-twenty-five thousand was a step in the right direction."

"I don't care about money. I just want to have Tugger alive again. This waiting will be hard to endure."

"We will just have to apply ourselves more diligently to your education, so that you will be a fitter companion to the Book of Forgetting when he arrives."

And indeed, despite Klom's anxiousness and impatience, the thirteen days that Nomar Zabumba had stipulated passed in a not altogether oppressive fashion. Klom's lessons were supplemented by excursions to local tourist sites, such as the Flame Falls and the extensive parklands centred on the Battlefield of the Pregnant Virgins. The pair took all their meals at an open-air stand not far from the hotel that specialised in bowls of noodle soup larded with one's choice of cubed planimal meats.

At last the promised day of Tugger's full instantiation arrived. Checking in from the hotel with the strandcrafter, Lingle verified that delivery would indeed occur at the stipulated time. Klom had them waiting at the shop in Morgay Prospect an hour ahead of their appointment. But they found the door locked, and so Klom paced anxiously while Lingle occupied himself playing some recondite boardgame with a passel of elderly Leatherheads sitting in a small park, their distinctive skulls all buffed to a high sheen.

Finally the outer door unlocked itself and the customers were allowed inside the shop.

The inner door opened as they entered, and Zabumba emerged.

Behind him trotted a fully mature Tugger, identical from antenna to paws to Klom's dear foundling.

Klom let out an exultant whoop and pushed past the Pryle gene-artisan. He fell to his knees and hugged the bulky creature. But Tugger – this avatar of him – made no sign of recognition, no gesture of joy, nor gave even an instinctive animal response by tongue or throat or tail. He seemed almost imperceptive and unprocessing of his environment: a zombie.

Klom got slowly to his feet and turned to Zabumba.

"What is the matter? Why isn't he friendly, or even really aware of me?"

Zabumba's non-human face conveyed regret and dismay as far as was possible.

"There were always two possibilities for this reincarnation. The being could emerge as a blank slate, a new entity with a natal brain-mind gestalt entirely unconnected to the life experiences of his predecessor. This would be the case if you or I were to be cloned. Baseline infantilism. But with a twelvestrand organism, I suspected – and hoped – that rebooting his carnal form would call down his soul from the deva dimensions, to fill and overlay the wetware."

"Explain further," Lingle urged.

"Well, of course you know that given your friend's ultra-dense and recomplicated genome, he should exist only in the higher deva dimensions. Instead, he's stable on our plane of reality. Nonetheless, I theorised that his soul had its basis and anchors in the deeper realities, and so that when his prior mortal form was snuffed, his severed quintessence remained intact, but outside our ken. I had hoped that reinstantiating his fleshly anchor would have served as a lure for the return of his soul. But instead there appears to be some failure to reconnect, leaving him neither inhabited nor full of naïve potential."

"This seems a sensible theory. But why did the reconnection not happen?"

"A matter beyond my expertise. For that answer, I suggest you consult a marabout. I can recommend one highly… Oh, and here is your genome fiche." The Pryle handed it over. "I must admit that I tried to copy its contents – just for academic purposes, you understand – and it self-destructed. I should have known that the boffins at Radius Seven would engineer such a protective feature. So your only source of this being's code is now the being itself."

Klom glared at Zabumba, but forebore from accusing him of duplicity. Having Tugger back, even in this partial manner, excused the strandcrafter's excess.

Discovering that the uninspired Tugger would respond to simple prodding, Klom and Lingle managed to exit the strandcrafter's shop with their new witless child. They had to summon a four-seater tuk-tuk to carry the hefty beast, who required Klom's leverage under his butt to clamber into the vehicle.

The small, colourfully painted columned temple on Windmaul Street diffused saltspray-tinged incense out its open door. Offerings from local citizens lay heaped at either side of the entrance. Klom and Lingle managed to herd Tugger inside. In the shadowy space they disturbed the marabout at an arcane ritual near the iconostasis, involving ewer, basin, hypersonic sounding rod and stochastic prayer paddles. A small water sprite danced in the bowl, yipping in an unknown tongue.

The officiant belonged to the race known as the Friment, whose genderless members resembled squat oblate cones with their sensory organs near their crowns; one multi-jointed limb splitting into two manipulators; and jaundice-coloured, waffle-textured epidermis. Clad in a sigil-spattered translucent robe that covered them from narrow flattened top down to broad flexible uni-ped base, the marabout dismissed the sprite, which fell apart into molecules of the host liquid, ending its performance, and turned to the visitors.

"I am Presbyter Przl. What spiritual hunger drives you into our embrace today?"

Klom said, "We need to know where to find the soul of our friend here."

Presbyter Przl palpated Tugger's body from head to tail, evoking no response from the creature. "Yes, yes, a vitanul. His essence is elsewhere." They humped themselves to a cabinet and removed a cranial netting connected by a single cable to a detector box featuring multiple readouts. Draping the netting atop Tugger's boulder-like skull, the marabout activated the machine and began to fiddle with the controls. They studied the display intently for a full fifteen minutes, then removed the netting, tucked away the whole assemblage, and confronted Klom and Lingle.

"This is the empty shell of a deva unlike any I have ever heard of or encountered."

"We know that!" Klom said. "But we need to find his soul."

"Do you know the concept of *terma?* A hidden teaching or treasure. Insofar as I can determine, the standard three parts of your deva's soul – the *ib*, the *ka* and the *ba* – have been separated by the shock of death and taken up residence far apart as *terma*. These are not, of course, physical objects, but rather higher-dimensional matrical resonances tethered each to a particular world by synchronised lock-in of vibrational planes."

Lingle inquired, "And if we brought our friend to these special planets?"

"I believe that with expert guidance from one of my peers residing in each *terma* location, the components could be made to reinhabit his mortal frame. Upon the third world he would become once more complete."

Klom wanted to shake information out of the marabout much faster, but held back. "Where are these worlds? Which planets do we have to visit? And how can we contact the local marabouts?"

"Reaching out to my colleagues is a simple matter. I can provide you with contact specifics. But first I must make the attempt to discover the locations of the *terma*. Of course, I must risk my own sensibilities and employ rare holy resources that require frequent replenishing…"

Klom sent money to the temple's account, and Presbyter Przl immediately assembled incense, drugs, a tray of Frillgill sacrificial amphibians, and a majestic robe. With many invocations, mantras and mudras, the marabout began to scry.

Nearly an hour later, Przl emerged from their far-seeing fugue and, in a voice made raw by chanting, offered three names.

"Alnair Grus 7, Oksanax, Voyle. Here be the *terma* three."

Lingle put a small paw on Klom's wide hand. "Those names are familiar somehow… *Khun* Bravalo, let us look at your triptix."

Lingle slotted the palette into the reader and scrolled to the next three prearranged destinations, the last stops between Stratcom and Mount Sumeru.

Alnair Grus 7, Oksanax, Voyle.

And the name of the first destination was already flashing, with departure of the luxury-class wavepacket *Penhaligon* scheduled for just two hours from now.

Returning to their hotel and assembling their belongings took nearly half the allotted time before departure, mainly due to having to wrestle with Tugger's mute inertia. But at last Klom and Lingle stood with their trunks and Tugger on the sidewalk, awaiting the hired ride to the port.

Anxious and impatient, Klom said, "What could be delaying our driver?"

Lingle looked perplexed. "I don't know… Have you noticed that the street is emptying of people?"

Klom registered that the busy citizens of this district had all retreated inside, and that vehicles had ceased flowing down the avenue. But before he could offer a guess about the phenomenon, the reason for the flight of the innocents was made plain.

From the direction of the soaring, gleaming towers that were home to Stratcom's portion of the terabase elite, a figure came floating through the sky, upborne by his swarm of majestatics. Cruising at an altitude of a dozen metres, the multistrand being, at first just a hazy dot, soon dropped to about twice the height of Klom's head and assumed recognisable configurations.

A Gorgoid by species, the entity was bipedal, reptilian, twice the size of Klom. It flaunted large ribbed membranous ears, a spike-studded tail and shell-plated back, with its soft ventral side protected by moulded armour; otherwise it wore no clothing. As it came closer, it grinned to show a plethora of formidable sharp teeth.

Klom's grip went instinctively for the watercutter pistol that used to hang always at his side, with which he had dealt so effectively with Bright Tide Rising's threat. But of course his instinctive thrust was stymied.

The multistrand lordling had arrived, holding apart a few metres and floating with its bare scaly clawed feet at a level just above Klom's head.

"My name is Truth's Abstract Smile. I am here to assume possession of your twelvestrand charge."

Klom's temper flared. "Again! What right do you have to take him? Tugger's not property, he's a free creature!"

"I assert ancient provenance over The Book of Forgetting. Although long lost, he was created by my species more than a millennium ago, to ensure that our natural rule over genetically less fortunate races should never be successfully challenged. Let me be frank with you. We terabases are relatively few, you know, compared to your teeming trillions. So we needed the Book's powers of reordering reality. He is a potent weapon beyond anything you can imagine, and you and your peers are incapable of safeguarding or deploying him wisely."

"He's not a weapon, he's my friend. And you can't have him! Get rid of your cloud of killer bugs, then come down here face to face. I'll fight you for him!"

Truth's Abstract Smile grinned in a display of many sharp teeth shining in his stubby snout. "Much as I would enjoy such a frivolous and brief tussle, I decline your offer."

"Then what are you waiting for? Just kill me and Lingle, take Tugger and be gone! I'll haunt you forever! You and your greedy, ruthless kind! I killed one of you already, you know, on Asperna. And I'll do the same to you if I get a chance."

"Yes, we know about your lucky assassination of Bright Tide Rising. But, again frankly, that Horseface was an incompetent idiot. Why do you think he was assigned to your miserable world? It was the only task he was suited for, running a junkyard. You may find an assault against any other one of our kind less successful."

Klom raised a huge fist. "Do your worst then, and be damned."

The tableau persisted for aching seconds that seemed an eternity. Klom felt poor Lingle quivering against his leg, and from the corners of his vision he sensed furtive fearful movements from behind window shutters as the citizenry awaited the destruction of this big stranger who had dared to antagonise and resist one of the high multistrand caste.

Klom's consciousness was blank of ideations, just a seething ocean of fear and anger, jealousy and vindictiveness, protectiveness and rage. But then a revelation washed over him, and he laughed enormously.

"You can't take him! Something's stopping you. If you could grab Tugger you would've done it already, just drilled us without a word and made off with him. So all your threats are empty."

Truth's Abstract Smile frowned, and his self-important lustre seemed to dim a fraction.

"Very bright you are, especially for a simpleton. Yes, this is correct. The Book of Forgetting seems to radiate a protective noosphere around himself and you that precludes harm. Not all harm, of course. A falling boulder could still bash your head in. But intentionally malign qualia emanating from any sentience are negated. All part and parcel of the Book's multiversal phase-changing abilities. Do you understand any of this? No, of course not. What a bloody waste."

"So it's a stalemate. Fine by me! What're you going to do?"

"I could imprison the three of you, let you all rot until you decided to cooperate. I think there's a good chance that the Book's instinctive protections would not interpret such a move to incarcerate as inimical. But I believe you would rather die than surrender. And since the Book himself is still mindless and soulless and in a diminished state, he might expire as well. No, that would be a fruitless course. So I am going to let you go about your business – with this message. You will never be out of the sight of me and my peers, even if you do not see us. You will never be truly secure or safe. At any moment we might find a way to pierce your protection or separate you all from each other. You will never be sure who is a friend and who is one of our agents. So try to endure those nervewracking conditions for a while, and maybe you will change your mind and surrender the Book. And consider this, as a carrot to the stick: your instant intransigence has not yet allowed me to make you an offer for your voluntary cooperation. We can be extremely generous. A whole world can be yours, title conveyed and sealed, if you simply relinquish this dumb beast."

"Take your world and choke on it!"

"So be it. For the moment."

Truth's Abstract Smile instantly rocketed up and away, becoming a mere pinprick in the sky in seconds.

Klom felt immense relief, however conditioned. The stink of an instant flopsweat suddenly poured off him. He looked first to Tugger, who had maintained his imperturbable blank stance throughout, a thread of drool hanging from one jowl. Then he cast his gaze at Lingle.

The little Vib had collapsed to the pavement in a faint. Klom lifted him up and laid him on one of their trunks. The locals now flooded out of hiding, shouting and celebrating Klom's victory. A friendly drink vendor pressed a pod of flavoured water into Klom's hand, and he got some down Lingle's throat and splashed the rest on his furry face.

Lingle came to.

"I am extremely sorry for my incapacity, *Khun* Bravalo! I promise you, it won't happen again!"

"Ling, you just beat me to the collapse. I was ready to fall all in a heap."

"Nonsense! You were a pillar of strength!"

"I would never have had the wit or courage to talk back to that bastard without your educating me, Ling."

Lingle hopped off the trunk. "Says the fellow who previously chopped up a lordling into bloody chunks. Here's our ride now. Hurry, or we'll miss our ship!"

The *Penhaligon* was the most luxurious ship that Klom had yet voyaged on since leaving Asperna, rich with sensual fabrics, woods, mosaics and other organics veneering its sophisticated technological armature. Buying passage for Lingle and Tugger had consequently chewed up a hefty portion of his monies. Some five kilometres from bow to stern, and with proportionate dimensions along its other axes, the *Penhaligon* carried ten thousand travellers in plush comfort. The passengers were heading for a variety of destinations, with Alnair Grus 7 being one of the lesser ports, some three weeks travel from Stratcom. They constituted a deep tranche of the Indrajal's many races, cultures, societies and castes, offering perplexing, alluring, disturbing customs, rituals, modes of thought and behaviour, each individual journeying for reasons frivolous, ceremonial, vocational, or mystical.

Klom broke out his fanciest clothing for daily interaction with his fellows. Lingle too assumed his best outfits. Tugger remained passive in their cabin, requiring no food, just a little water, in the same metabolically enigmatic fashion that the original Tugger had manifested back on Asperna.

At first, Klom had been reluctant to get very far apart from the Book, for fear of exiting that sphere of protection which Truth's Abstract Smile had outlined. But Lingle did some research into similar phenomena – most notably among the communally bonded Crinoids of Glyphenhalle – and affirmed that such mutual dependence was not a function of proximity in four-dimensional space, but rather derived from sub-aetheric connections.

"So long as our psychic affinity bonds remain intact, we need not lie atop each other for safety. I trust my devotion to our cause protects me."

"And since I could never *not* love Tugger, even in his sad condition, we are all set!"

Reassured, Klom (with Lingle generally by his side, save when the little Vib attended to personal pleasures and religious duties), resolved to make the most of his expensive passage. All thoughts of what the future might bring were put aside – not actually a hard task for the stolid, close-horizoned and unanxious Klom. After dutifully blocking out several hours each day to continue his education, he exercised in the ship's gym and swam endless lengths in both the fresh- and salt-water pools, often sharing his lane with a school of sinuous cowled Ommastrephes. That is, until the family was banned from the pool when a juvenile accidently let loose a copious inky discharge.

After a life of paucity, Klom regarded the limitless cosmopolitan buffets as a personal challenge, and was willing to try anything billed as edible for humans – and some items deemed otherwise – at least once. He found many congenial table partners who expressed honest vicarious admiration for Klom's eating prowess. Many meals transitioned into boozy singalongs and table-top dancing – officially frowned on by the stewards, who were nonetheless placated by large tips.

One couple who sat apart from the common festivities intrigued Klom.

The male of the pair was human or human-adjacent and nearly as massive as Klom. Either congenitally or through some kind of infection, his entire bluish epidermis, including shaved skull, was tessellated with hard warts the size and shape of the small trapezoid biscuits Klom's mother had often baked, back at Lake Zawinul. The man's permanent expression was a belligerent scowl.

His partner, a woman, registered incontrovertibly as a chimera with human and animal components. Her white, not unattractive face was longish, with a broad flat nose and widely spaced dark eyes. Barefoot, she wore an unvarying black outfit of simple stretchy bandeau and loose trunks which revealed that her entire body was covered with a tight curly nap of cream-colored wool. Her countenance was an invariant mask of acceptance overlaid on sorrow. Or so Klom thought, having seen the identical look on many of his fellow salvage yard citizens.

After some discreet inquiries with the purser, Lingle made a report, recounting his findings in the privacy of their cabin, as Klom absentmindedly petted the unresponsive Tugger.

"The man is Ludes Kedgrigorn. He hails from Mabune, where until recently he was a foreclosure agent for a bio-camorra. Whenever a freelance member of the criminal organisation became derelict in his payments for any type of augmentation, Kedgrigorn would track him down and reclaim the proprietary organ or prosthetic or enhancement. This quite often resulted in the very messy demise of the defaulter."

"What is he doing on the *Penhaligon*? Is he tracking down some runaway debtor for his false teeth?"

"Not at all. It appears that *Khun* Kedgrigorn has retired from his violent line of work. The boss of the bio-camorra was discovered recently lacking his head, and the organisation's treasury had been emptied. *Khun* Kedgrigorn's surly disposition may be attributed to his entirely legitimate fears regarding pursuit and retribution. Having paid a huge amount to the security experts on the asylum world of Beschloss for a well-guarded estate, he must reach that refuge before he can breathe easy again."

"And what of the girl?"

"She is a simple off-the-shelf bondswoman named Olasia. She was one of his last purchases before leaving Mabune. There seems to be little involved in their relationship other than carnal satisfaction for Kedgrigorn."

Klom pondered this information. "He's a bad man, a criminal on the run. I don't like it. Especially him dragging that innocent girl along with him."

"Certain authorities might regard you in the same light. After all, you did kill a lordling and flee justice."

Klom jumped to his feet, anger evident in his knotted fists and rageful face. "Only in self-defence, after he had murdered three of my innocent friends!"

"Be calm! I know all that. I was just playing devil's advocate! The point I am trying to make is that we cannot set ourselves up as judge and jury in this case. Despite his crimes, Kedgrigorn has somehow obtained legal passage on this ship, and we are not representatives of any law-enforcement agency."

"Still, I will watch him closely for some chance to make things right."

"As you wish. But don't jeopardise our own mission."

The next day Klom began to shadow Kegrigorn in what he hoped was a non-obtrusive manner. The fellow generally emerged from his quarters close to eleven in the shiptime morning, just before the breakfast selections were to be cleared away. Shortly after a large meal he began drinking intoxicating beverages steadily, though never to the point of debilitation. He would occasionally play a card game called 'pitch and ditch', wagering small sums with the assembled strangers and denying their attempts at conversation. For evening's entertainment he favoured the lugubrious wailing of a cabaret singer from Audax, a batrachian being with enormous resonant throat pouch.

Most of the time Olasia was forced to accompany her owner. She did so meekly, but with a quiet dignity.

Kedgrigorn's liquor intake sent him on frequent trips to the lavatory, and at these times he left Olasia alone, waiting patiently in the public rooms for his return

Klom took advantage of one such occasion to approach the chimera as she sat on a low stool placed next to Kedgrigorn's more comfortable lounge chair. Her posture expressed resignation and alertness for any orders.

"*Khun* Olasia."

She regarded Klom with her deep-pooled hyperteloric eyes. Her voice was soft, her articulation not precisely human. "You name me strangely. I am just Olasia. No title for my kind. How may I be of service?"

"Does he abuse you?"

"My owner? I must do whatever he wishes."

"But there are laws regarding the proper treatment of bondspeople. You are not private property, just rentals."

"I do not know about laws. I only know some behaviours are approved, and some behaviours are punished."

"This should not be. If you need help any time, just come to me."

"No one can help me."

"You are wrong." Klom looked toward the lavatories and saw Kedgrigorn emerging. "I must go. Just remember what I said."

Klom retreated across the room. Kedrigorn eyed him suspiciously, while Klom feigned a bumbling, smiling innocence. The outlaw from Mabune leaned in close to Olasia and began to question her with a low-voiced fierceness. Abruptly, he grabbed her by the arm, yanked her to her feet, and they departed the salon.

The next day Olasia appeared with the fur of one cheek barely concealing a livid contusion flaring on the pink skin beneath. She looked away when she saw Klom.

Feeling awful, Klom did not know what he could do to make the girl's situation better, and feared to make it worse. For once, Lingle had no advice.

For the next several days Klom maintained his interest at an unprovocative distance from the pair. He had time to ponder his motives. Although nothing like the lamented Sorrel – fiery, headstrong, impetuous – Olasia conjured up similar feelings of protectiveness and affection in Klom's giant mute heart. He did not seek to source or analyse these emotions or manage them. Their simple existence provided enough justification. Klom trusted his inner guides.

But Klom's attitude of discreet watchfulness received a blow on the morning when Olasia was seen supporting a homeostatic cast on what proved to be a fractured arm. Once again, Lingle, through pumping the ship's medico assigned to their quadrant of the vast ship, learned the dirt.

"Kegrigorn's liquor consumption passed all normal bounds last night, rousing him to loud belligerence and complaints, and when Olasia tried to steer him back to their room, he lashed out at her."

Klom fumed. "This cannot stand."

"What do you propose?"

"I will batter him to a pulp!"

"And then what of our quest? Nothing will avail when you are clamped in the brig, awaiting official charges at our next port, perhaps with your true identity exposed."

Calming down, Klom said, "There must be some way to free Olasia."

"Of course, her indenture would revert to the Indrajal agency responsible for bondspeople if her owner died – an unlikely eventuality, for surely you don't intend to murder him."

"No, of course not!"

"Maybe you could convince the ruffian to sell her to you…"

"I'll try it!"

The next day Klom approached the ex-enforcer when the man seemed somewhat lulled by his first three drinks of the day. Olasia had, apparently, been left in their room. Anxious to attain his goal, Klom avoided all pleasantries.

"*Khun* Kedgrigorn, I want to make a deal with you. Give me your bondmaid's lease, and I'll pay you three times what you paid. I've taken a fancy to her, that's all."

The big Mabunian studied Klom with a sober and calculating intensity tinged with ire and jealousy. "I've seen you carousing with all these swells. You're as ugly as me, but that doesn't seem to matter. They're happy for your company. *Khun* Bravalo, the mingy juice-monger! But I'm not good enough for society. Too scary, hands too dirty, even though I'm worth more than most. You could bed any of those posh bints if you wanted. So why so interested in my little toy lamb?"

Klom could make no answer. Kegrigorn said, "Go away, and don't bother me again." He returned to his drink.

After hesitating a moment, fists bunched, Klom left.

But the affair was taken out of Klom's hands and settled the next evening, in what was perhaps an inevitable incident, given Kedgrigorn's surliness.

Klom and Lingle occupied a table in the Topaz Room with three or four spontaneous comrades. Dance music issued from a trio on stage, and servitors brisked through the room with drinks and delicious-smelling snacks. Across the salon brooded Kedgrigorn, alone save for a downcast Olasia seated by his knees on her stool. She rubbed her cast as if to solace the wound beneath. Klom bristled to see her sad discomfort.

Into the room swept a jubilant party of three Wolonines. The oversized fanged and tailed bipeds featured idiosyncratic dye jobs of their shaggy pelts, and an assortment of barbaric quasi-rhodium piercings on ears, nose and lips. Each was accompanied by a bondscreature whose main duty, it seemed, was to make sure the flagons of their masters never went dry, replenishing from leather bota bags.

One of the alien servants – they resembled Lingle if the Vib had been morphed with an awkward aquatic bird – spotted Olasia and called out a greeting in chimeric creole. Olasia perked up and actually smiled. The bouncy Wolonine servant hastened to her side.

Kedgrigorn's attention was roused from glowering over his drink. When the intruder got within range, Kedgrigorn kicked out savagely and sent the squealing bondscreature hurtling, amber liquid spraying from its bota.

The Wolonine trio came to an immediate halt. Alien countenances did not duplicate human emotions, but their immense displeasure was nonetheless apparent. The musicians tapered off playing within seconds, and all the dancers paused as if frozen in place.

The three big bipeds moved to surround Kedgrigorn. He got hastily to his feet, realising too late his mistake. Olasia skittered backwards on her stool.

One of the Wolonines spoke. "Deliver amends now, or prepare to fight."

Kedgrigorn manifested belligerence. "You make too much of the simple exercise of my superior rights as a free sapient. I simply kicked some trash out of my path."

"No words. Pay, grovel, or die!"

Kedgrigorn sized up the unarmed Wolonines. He seemed to reach for a fiche-reader hanging from his belt, as if to transfer funds. But then suddenly a sharpfinger leaped into his hand, and was flicked instantly alive. A thin whistling wind sounded, as air was sucked through the weapon into some distant vacuum. The cruel blade of the knife was spotted along its length with flickering mirror-shiny microscale matter-modem dots. As the blade plunged into its victim, portions of whatever it encountered would be in effect surgically removed by the on-off working of the dots, and then transported some hundreds of kilometres away. Not to any matching output modem, but rather via randomised white hole pathways – essentially into the interstellar vacuum, given the *Penhaligon*'s location. This must have been, Klom realised, the tool of the repossessor's former trade.

"Now we'll see who grovels! Or would you rather just run away!"

"Neither," growled one of the Wolonines. Fearless, the alien moved faster than Klom could apprehend, and Kedgrigorn was suddenly leaking seemingly non-fatal amounts of blood. The blue warty human looked in blank astonishment to see the sharpfinger handle protruding from his own chest. Then he collapsed to the sloppy floor, as his innards were siphoned into the void.

Screams, tumult, the crashing of overturned furniture. Lingle was nowhere to be seen, but Klom remained steadfast at his table.

When the ship's security officials eventually appeared on the run – not tardily, by any objective measure, but after a subjective eternity – Kedgrigorn was dead beyond recovery.

Klom approached the group standing around the body.

Displaying a document on his reader, one of the Wolonines said, "Diplomats, we. All relevant Indrajal courtesy and protections. Sufficient, yes?"

The head of the responders, a lanky Foambone, studied the credentials, then agreed. "Yes, fine, no legal charges. But you will have to pay for the cleanup."

"Understood."

The Wolonines left festively then, seeking to continue their celebrations in a less-messy salon. The head of the security team removed the weapon, remarkably clean, from the corpse and deactivated it. An overturned goblet trickled its contents drop by drop with surprising loudness amidst the stunned silence.

Klom spoke to the Foambone. "The bondswoman. What becomes of her?"

Her eyes wide but unfocused, Olasia sat quivering in the lee of an overturned table, her white wool dotted with some of her former master's blood.

"She will go into a suspensor-sac until we arrive at our next stop, where she will be turned over to the proper agency."

"Could I buy her lease now?"

The officer consulted with someone on the other end of his communicator. "Yes, of course, we have the power to register the transferal temporarily, until arrival."

Seemingly appearing from nowhere, Lingle now stood once more by Klom's side. "You'll excuse me, *Khun* Bravalo, but when that contretemps erupted, I felt my survival and hence my continued service would be best ensured by a swift removal to a more secure corner of the ship."

"I understand, Ling. Now, please give these folks our information so we can buy Olasia."

The transaction was concluded swiftly, and the security men helped Olasia to her feet and presented her to Klom.

"I suggest," said the Foambone, "that you bring her to the medico for a dose of calmative. We will transfer any of her luggage from *Khun* Kedrigorn's cabin to yours."

Klom gently took hold of Olasia's arm. "Come with me now, and all will be well."

The shocked chimera did not exhibit any hesitancy or eagerness, but seemed almost as will-less as the current avatar of Tugger. She allowed herself to be led away by Klom, Lingle following solicitously.

After the dispensary visit, they all returned to the cabin.

Tugger remained in his usual recumbent posture, a jowly boulder, forepaws folded beneath him, an empty shell kept going on autonomic functioning alone.

Lingle said, "Shall I have the stewards install a cot? Or do you intend for this creature to share your bed?"

Klom's face grew hot. "Her own cot, of course."

It took half an hour to get the expando-foam crib delivered and set up. Klom used that time to introduce Olasia to Tugger. Although the insensate Book of Forgetting made no overtures when Klom drew Olasia's lax hand repeatedly across his rump, the simple physical contact seemed to soothe her. By the time her bed was ready, she seemed much more composed and rational, although showing the effects of the calmative. After climbing into the crib and drawing the blankets up almost over her face, she granted Klom a look of cautious gratitude.

With lights dimmed, Klom stretched out on his own extra-large mattress. Blissful unconsciousness eluded him. He pondered the vast disjunction in his life that the past few weeks had brought. From a hovel on Asperna, with Sorrel, Airey and a sprightly Tugger, to this cabin hurtling at lightspeed through the galaxy, with a Vib, a chimera and a blank-souled twelvestrand. When the disparity of circumstances and the vector of destiny they limned became too much to contemplate, Klom finally surrendered to sleep.

When Klom awoke, Olasia's bed showed empty. (Lingle still emitted chirring snores.) Klom experienced a moment's alarm until she emerged from the bathroom, wearing her typical outfit. The specks of blood on her coat had been washed away, and her fawn-like eyes exhibited a lively curiosity. Klom took pleasure at evidence of her resilience.

"Master –"

"No, not Master. Sit. You probably don't know this, but before Kedgrigorn died, I tried to buy your contract from him. I resented the abuse he dumped on you. I've been stomped on all my life too. I thought I could make your life better. That's all. But he refused to sell you. Yet fate finally allowed me to have my way. So now you can consider yourself on vacation. And when your lease comes due again, we'll see what happens. My own future is too uncertain for me to promise more."

Olasia placed her small hand atop Klom's. "I want to be of service in any way I can. Tell me how. Say what I must do."

"Well, I'm on a mission. It involves Tugger." Klom provided a simplified history of himself and the Book of Forgetting. "If you want to come along and assist us – be an extra pair of eyes in strange places, provide some good cheer – then that would be all I ask."

"I don't understand everything. But your mission sounds honourable and important. I will do all I can to help."

Her hand warm on his, Klom gazed into Olasia's depthless eyes for what seemed a long time – until Lingle spoke.

"One prerequisite for any success in this mad quest is actually to leave the room and get some nourishment. Unless you believe you can subsist on moonbeam gazes alone."

Kedgrigorn's body was offloaded at the very next port, far from the asylum world of Beschloss where his elite freehold offering security and protection would go untenanted – unless he had some heir who could lay claim to his dangerous legacy of stolen riches. As Klom watched the suspensor-sac concealing Kedrigorn's corpse being floated offship, he reflected on the unknowable nature of any man's future. Could the Mabunian have predicted this ignominious burial far from home? Likewise, could Klom foresee what lay around the corner of his own path? He hoped to resurrect Tugger, but then what? Would Truth's Abstract Smile and his terabase peers simply allow Klom and Tugger to live on some backwater world in peace? Not very likely. How could Klom possibly wrest control of his own destiny away from such a powerful figure? The problem seemed insoluble, and so Klom just let it go.

Four days later, the *Penhaligon* arrived at Alnair Grus 7. The ship would be leaving immediately after unloading selected passengers, and Klom and his party would continue onward later aboard the equally amenable *Varanaryan*, which had yet to arrive at Alnair Grus 7. That is, assuming they could accomplish what they needed to do first.

Alnair Grus 7 was a gas dwarf, a type of planet that resided midway between the rocky habitable worlds and gas giants without any solid cores. Its gravity rated one-point-five times the most comfortable human norm, and so any visitor who desired help with this unaccustomed burden was equipped with a personal belt-mounted floater unit with variable offset controls. Klom opted out, making the same decision for Tugger, while Lingle and Olasia gratefully accepted the aid.

The planet boasted only a single domed city, Maybloom, known far and wide across the Indrajal as a honeymoon destination. The turbulent polychromatic atmosphere of the planet, wracked by the most dramatic lightning-riven storms, afforded a constant romantic background of high emotional drama, while the hostile environment conduced otherwise towards indoor pleasures between or among partners. But Maybloom also possessed many fine restaurants, casinos and other sophisticated amusements.

On the surface the shuttlecraft bearing Klom and his friends mated with a tunnel airlock at some distance from the dome, and soon they were walking with their fellow disembarkers in gawping astonishment, separated from the swirling electric crayola skies by only a transparent tunnel roof.

Once inside the dome proper, Lingle found them a relatively inexpensive hotel within walking distance. At the reception desk, the human-adjacent clerk, a Heruka female with enormous fangs and painted claws, inquired of Klom.

"*Khun* Bravalo, we have a lovely assortment of suites ready for your enjoyment. I only need to know the type of sleeping arrangements desired."

"What do you mean?"

The veteran clerk remained nonchalant. "Would you like a bed for four? A triplet and a single? Two doubles? Or some other setup I have regretably failed to consider?"

Flustered, Klom replied, "Three singles, please. Tugger doesn't need one."

The clerk's bushy magenta eyebrow twitched almost imperceptibly. "But of course."

83

Up in their room, Olasia said, "I don't need my own bed either, you know. Especially if it costs extra. I can sleep on the floor next to Tugger. Or share with Lingle. He's only as big as the fuzzy Artificial Mama we used to snuggle with in the creche."

Klom laughed, and now it was the Vib's turn to be embarrassed. "Nonsense! I have restless leg syndrome and kick all night like an irate pack animal. Sleep in Klom's bed if you want to save us a few taka. I have observed that he passes the whole nocturnal period as motionless as mountain."

Olasia smiled. "That might not be the case if I slept with him."

Klom experienced an unsettling mix of emotions. "Enough of this crazy talk!" he ordered. "We need to find the marabout that Presbyter Przl named for us."

After a few necessary ablutions, the trio left the hotel room. Klom had decided not to bring Tugger until they had encountered the marabout and confirmed his willingness to perform the necessary rituals to reunite the *ba* portion of Tugger's numinous body with his shell.

The temple occupied a tiny storefront wedged between a stochastic pachinko parlour and a strandcrafter specialising in 'physio-harmonisation for lovers'. Klom and his companions entered, and discovered the place's generic resemblance to the temple on Stratcom and the millions of other dotted across the Indrajal.

Out from the private part of the building slithered a serpent-like being large enough to swallow Lingle and perhaps even Olasia at a single gulp: a member of the Sheshan race. Rearing half-ceilingward, the acolyte exhibited a flaring yellow-ribbed skin hood that folded open and shut behind its head. Without adornments, the creature was fitted with a set of prosthetic manipulators clamped around its upper body to compensate for its congenital lack of limbs.

The Sheshan's voice lacked the anticipated sibilance, and instead resembled the sound of a stick rasping across a gnurled nut. "I am Mufti Hodak. What twist of karma deposits you here today?"

Klom named Presbyter Przl and specified their mission. Hodak showed instant recognition.

"I have been anticipating your arrival. This is a most interesting phenomenon. I have been parsing the devic outfall leakage ever since I was informed of my task. Many puzzling qualia torrent upward from the implicate order. I believe that the devas of the higher dimensions deliberately sequestered the three parts of your mundane deva's soul. For what purpose I cannot say."

"Do you think they will hinder his reunion?"

"We will find out soon enough. Quickly now! Bring your friend here!"

Leaving his companions in the temple, Klom hurried to retrieve Tugger. Herding the Book of Forgetting through the crowded avenues full of unsuspecting romancers, he wondered what alterations might manifest in his friend's blank attitude if the procedure should succeed.

Mufti Hodak had arrayed all his necessary implements and a cageful of downy twitterlings as sacrifice. He reared up higher in excitement when Tugger arrived.

"Yes, yes, manifestly an empty vessel, totally bereft! We will reinsert the *ba* first, since that is the portion allocated psychically to this planetary nexus. My compeers on Oksanax and Voyle will deal with the *ka* and *ib*."

As strong fumes began to fill the temple and ineffable chants rang out, Klom, Lingle and Olasia hung back at a safe distance from Tugger and the Mufti.

Tugger stood stolidly amidst coruscations and invocations both. At last the ceremony was completed. Hodak slumped the lax upper portion of his body across a low cabinet as if utterly drained from his exertions.

"The attachment is complete. My part in this enigma is fulfilled. Go now."

Klom advanced toward Tugger – and Tugger, though still expressionless, stepped forward of his own initiative! Klom flung himself around the neck of his massive friend, expecting the old familiar slobbering kisses. None came, and Klom's heart crashed. He peered intently into the wrinkled face. Was there a slight gleam of rekindled spirit in Tugger's eyes? Any hint of recognition? Perhaps. But not yet enough.

Outside the temple, the foursome ambled toward the hotel. Tugger's newly restored facilities seemed to incline him to follow without being chivvied. The broad thronged avenue they followed featured an unbroken line of buildings on their left, but only the naked, gently curving shell of the city dome on their right, affording a spectacular vista of deadly cold and unbreathable gases.

"We have a day before we leave on the *Varanaryan*," said Klom, looking to his servant. "What can we do?"

Lingle began to answer, but stopped in mid-sentence. Klom took his eyes away from the Vib to see why.

Motionless in the air, swarmed by scintillant majestatics, Truth's Abstract Smile plainly awaited their arrival. The merciless lacertilian face of the multistrand lordling boded no good fortune.

The Gorgoid said, "You have embarked on a very unwise course. Already your attempted resurrection of the Book of Forgetting stirs currents across the whole Indrajal. And you imagine you are safe, simply because my actions cannot impinge on you directly. But that prohibition may be finessed, I have come to believe. Nothing stops me from altering your environment in some very dangerous ways. Please regard my actions now as a kindly warning not to proceed to your next destination. Merely depart this world without the Book, and all strife between us will be at an end."

Before Klom could reply, a portion of the attendant shoal peeled off, majestatics attaching themselves to the dome near the base.

Then they instantly disassembled a hole about a metre across in the protective wall.

The atmospheric pressure outside was vastly greater than that inside, so a raging river of methane and helium rushed in.

Above the atmospheric roaring came screams, scuffling, swearing, shouts.

Klom staggered against the invisible frigid assault of atmosphere, but did not fall. He saw Lingle lifted off his feet. But the Vib reacted swiftly and threw his arms around Tugger's foreleg, and held tight to that immovable bastion.

Olasia, however, was not so fortunate. The gale lifted her up, and with a wail she smashed into the high branches of an ornamental tree in its large pot. The foliage thrashed in the wind, the pot teetered, and her grip seemed destined to break. Loosened, she would slam hard against a building.

Klom ripped the floater belt off Lingle's waist and punched its simple controls. Instantly he was half his weight. He let the wind take him and he sailed also into the tree, bruising hard against its trunk. Clambering upward, he reached Olasia and snapped the buckle of her belt. Her floater mechanism dropped away, and he discarded his too. Subject to the planet's full gravity, she and he could better resist the noxious, choking gale. Klom gripped her tightly and prepared to leap down off the tree – then jumped.

Before he hit pavement, the alien wind ceased.

City repair mechanisms had clustered at the break, and applied at least a temporary seal.

Klom tried to set Olasia upon her own two feet, but she refused to loosen the grip of her arms around his neck, the clutch of her legs around his waist. Klom let her shiver out her fears. Her former master murdered before her eyes, and now the incomprehensible affairs of her current 'protector' exposing her to mortal attack. It would be enough to unnerve even the most stalwart soul.

At last Olasia unclenched and climbed down. Lingle limped over, registering both his increased weight and the effects of being pummelled by the gale. Imperturbable Tugger simply awaited direction.

Truth's Abstract Smile was nowhere to be seen. Not utterly above the law, perhaps even that sovereign potentate worried about being confronted by the authorities of Maybloom and charged with terrorism.

Lingle sat down cautiously on the sidewalk. "*Khun* Bravalo, it's your decision on how to proceed."

Klom regarded the unruffled Tugger, still two-thirds unrestored. He sized up Olasia and Lingle. Both returned his inspection with frank looks of confidence and faith.

"The demands of that dirty tera-bastard mean nothing!" said Klom. "We abandon no one. Onward to Oksanax!"

The next week's passage aboard the *Varanaryan* afforded everyone much-needed rest and recuperation – although overlain with some anxiety about how Truth's Abstract Smile would next attack them. Klom did not anticipate trouble aboard the starliner, for interstellar travel was too finicky a process to permit anything but fatal interference: no simple hijacking or detours possible. What point to sabotage their wavepacket ship if it meant that the irreplaceable Tugger ended up not in the lordling's grasp, but scattered as a cloud of particles across the unforgiving supraluminal medium?

But all activity on board was not mindless abandonment. Lingle insisted on continuing Klom's general studies, and Olasia sat in. Her caste-enforced ignorance of the Indrajal and its ways ran even deeper than Klom's, and he experienced for the first time in his life a sense of being possessed of greater sophistication than one of his companions. His days spent in complacent ignorance on Asperna seemed infinitely far away, a source of mild chagrin and bemusement. At the same time, he realised how much he continued not to comprehend. But at least he was moving in the right direction.

The chimera gradually became more at ease as one of their small posse, and unburdened herself of some of the insults to body and spirit that she had received at the hand of her old master. She spoke not vindictively, however, but matter-of-factly, and once she had shared an anecdote she never dwelled on it. Talk seemed to release any sorrow. When her cast came off her arm, she brightened even further. She was more apt to speak of happy times as a child in the creche. "We would tumble all over each other like a pack of Rafter pups, competing for extra snacks. Look, like this!"

Olasia would then demonstrate her slithery wrestling moves on the uncooperative Tugger and then, finding his lack of response unsatisfying, turn to Klom, who provided some competitive resistance, though always calibrating his strength against her slim form. The matches usually ended in sweaty, laughing collapse. Lingle held aloof, disdaining the exertions as unseemly, although Klom thought to detect a covert desire to participate.

Often these matches left Klom with a smoldering desire to possess Olasia as a woman, taking her as carefreely as he and Sorrel had once tumbled into each other's embrace. But he suppressed these urges and refrained.

By the time the ship arrived at Oksanax, Klom felt reinvigorated and ready for whatever their opponent might throw at them – assuming he had trailed them here or even anticipated their arrival, based perhaps on hacked intelligence of their triptix or even interrogation of Presbyter Przl. Maybe Tugger would exhibit some of his old formidability too, assuming the insertion of his *ka* could be achieved.

As they waited to offload from the *Varanaryan* – the *Maevelut's Pride* would carry them to Voyle three days from now – Lingle lectured on the nature of the new planet.

"Oksanax is a gaseous jovian world, and hence does not offer anything like a surface where one might set foot. Instead, a few floating city-resorts range throughout her upper atmosphere. They exist mainly to cater to the gem-hunting tourists. The atmospheric chemistry of this world promotes a steady rain of rubies and sapphires. Just as on some worlds you may with permission prospect for gold in a national park, so too here the visitor is allowed to bag his share of aerial gemstones. The process is a thrilling one. After a short virtual training session, an individual is dropped into a one-person sky sled equipped with exterior mechanical scoops. Slicing through the clouds, one spots a falling gem and then must maneuver one's craft to bag it. These approved methods are kept deliberately awkward and demanding, requiring some skill, so as not to result in industrial-level depletion of the gems. Occasionally a tourist will strike it rich by capturing an immense specimen. Occasionally, diving too deep into the atmosphere, a tourist will perish. But most just end up with thrills and a few tiny gems to show off back home."

"Oh," said Olasia, "I'd love to try that!"

"We'll see," said Klom. "Our first priority is to get Tugger's *ka* installed."

Crowded with others at the shuttle's broad panoramic window, Klom and his friends marvelled at the approach to the floating city-resort dubbed Dashaway. A huge transparent sphere with a thick interior plate at its equator, the habitat furnished antithetical gravities in each hemisphere, so that the central plate served as a floor for both sides. Half the buildings and people seemed unconcernedly upside-down to the tourists on the arriving shuttle. Although of course, once through the airlocks the visitor would experience a natural rightside-up orientation appropriate to that hemisphere.

Again Lingle found them satisfactory quarters, where they dropped their luggage and refreshed themselves. Feeling the pressure of time and possible intervention by Truth's Abstract Smile, Klom hastened them out in search of the temple that was expecting them. At the urgings of Lingle and Olasia, he permitted a stop for a meal, albeit just a bowl of greyfriar noodles and mantis meat. Tugger, who had never eaten much back on Asperna, still showed no appetite, a feature of his twelvestrand physiology.

The modest holy building sported a decorative striped onion dome atop a blocky base. A warbling threnody issued from speakers mounted above the door.

Inside the single room, harshly and colourfully illuminated as if to mimic an alien sun, they found Saltigue Mirzo. The officiant of the temple was a Threeple: a cask-like body, unclothed and unornamented, surmounted by a hemispherical head that could rotate almost three-hundred-and-sixty degrees before resuming its default orientation. Scattered sensory elements were merely darker spots on the viridian skin. The adept's mouth resembled the intake slot on a certain model of macerator Klom had used back on Asperna to break up ceramic insulators. A pair of legs and a pair of arms could be retracted inside the Threeple's torso when not needed.

Upon the arrival of Klom and party, Saltigue Mirzo extruded his lower limbs and strode toward the visitors. Klom introduced everyone and reminded Mirzo of their mission.

The Saltigue took down some type of metaphysical probe from a shelf and examined Tugger. The hologram readout flashed arcane symbols. "Yes, yes, just as I imagined. All the theoretical parameters obtain. The *ka* can be reslotted nicely." Mirzo began fussing then with a variety of other gadgets, affixing wires to Tugger by means of clips that pinched Tugger's perdurable hide.

Swiped on, the enlivened devices offered enough status lights to resemble a squad of fireflies. At last the Saltigue seemed ready to proceed.

Klom asked, "But where is the incense, the sacrifices?"

"Pah!" Mirzo replied. "The accoutrements of a superstitious past. This a branch of the Reform movement, and we do things the modern way here. Nonetheless, no layperson could channel the forces soon to be invoked. That numinous guidance requires decades of practice. Now, are you ready? Good, here we go!"

Mirzo tapped a control slate and a faint blue nimbus surrounded Tugger. The aura became host to a tangle of writhing golden threads. More and more rainbow worms invaded the space, weaving hypnotic patterns. Klom felt lost in a timeless zone. Then, with a simple pass, the array of machines was deactivated.

"Success," said Mirzo.

Klom studied Tugger intently, awaiting some new behaviour that would indicate a greater autonomy and individuality.

Tugger slowly raised a forepaw into his line of vision, studied it as if it were a foreign object belonging to someone else. Then, for the first time since his rebirth, the Book of Forgetting opened his jaws in a grin and let his tongue loll out.

Klom regarded this practically infantile behaviour as a minor miracle. He stroked Tugger's slab-like brow and the beast closed his mouth. Tugger's gaze, although not wholly ensouled, seemed to offer some additional facets of alertness and vivacity. Klom was pleased.

After transferring a large donation to the temple's accounts, Klom returned with his friends to the hotel.

"I intend us to hunker down here till departure time. It won't be fun, but it should be safe."

Olasia, still in her bandeau and shorts, said, "Do you think I might have some new clothes? This is my only outfit. I feel out of place in these fine quarters."

92

Klom felt sad and guilty that he had not considered Olasia's condition before now. New garments could have been purchased on the *Varanaryan.* "Of course. Lingle will go out with you to shop. He will know what clothes are proper."

The little Vib pretended to be put-upon, but Klom sensed some pride at his accreditation as a fashion expert.

The rest of that day and the next passed without incident. Meals and card games, naps and streamed entertainments filled the hours. From time to time Tugger would gnaw at an improbable itch, and that struck Klom as a marvellous sign.

With twenty-some hours left before departure, and no attack from Truth's Abstract Smile, Klom began to relax. Sensing this, Olasia asked, "Might we try to win some gems from the skies? It would be a little bit of real fun. We'll probably never pass this way again."

Klom considered, then asked Lingle, "What do you think?"

"It seems safe enough. Especially if I stay here with Tugger."

"All right then, let's go!"

Hangers housing the sky sled rentals dotted the periphery of Dashaway. They chose one at random, neither the closest nor the most distant. In this way, Klom hoped to foil anyone staking out the hangars in anticipation of their arrival. Such a manoeuvre seemed paranoid, but they had a real enemy.

The amusement-park atmosphere of the place conjured up a gaiety that Klom had not felt in ages, if ever. Tourists of all ages prepared eagerly for their brief jaunts through the gemstone rain of Oksanax. Olasia's excitement and joy were contagious. The training session included engrammatic and proprioceptive reinforcements, and Klom felt confident at his ability to handle the simple sky sled, which in truth had a number of safety protocols embedded in it to stop amateurs from actively killing themselves. The actual controls reminded him of several semi-complex tools he had operated at the salvage yard. Olasia expressed a similar faith in her training. And communications between their sleds would be constant.

Belly down on the cushions of the coffin-sized interiors, the transparent canopies secured above them, Klom and Olasia were launched out into the planet's ruby-seeded clouds.

The propulsion units of the sky sleds were quick and powerful, the manoeuvring vanes intuitive and responsive, and the grappler an arcade-worthy challenge. At the end of a long flexible piezo-muscled hollow arm was a cup with which to scoop up a falling gem. The prize was then impelled down the hollow tube into a catch-basin that could be unloaded back in the hanger.

Upon launching, Olasia immediately gunned her craft ahead of Klom's, cutting through the pastel fogs and whorls of Oksanax's upper atmosphere. The windshield of each craft featured a sizable display pane that gave an augmented reality image simulating from sensor information what might have been seen if the occluding gasses had not been present, and so Klom could keep an eye on Olasia's sled despite the reality of fluctuatingly opaque conditions.

Olasia shrieked. "I've got a stone! It's big as my pinky, I swear it!"

Klom shared Olasia's excitement and happiness. He was not even bothering to attempt to capture any drifting gems, content merely to abet Olasia's fun. "Wonderful! You can make a necklace out of them if you just get a few more."

By now they were a few kilometres away from the city sphere, with no other sleds nearby.

And thus Truth's Abstract Smile staged his appearance for them alone.

The large Gorgoid floated in the midst of the churning poisonous clouds protected by a force corona generated by his majestatics. Presumably, he could have contacted Klom through the sled's system had he wished to bluster or threaten, but he did not deign to do so.

94

Instead, he simply dispatched a portion of his swarm to shear off the vanes on Olasia's sled and kill her engines.

Down her craft began to plummet.

Her piercing shrieks this time were not of joy.

Instantly Klom kicked his sled into maximum acceleration. He caught up to Olasia's craft within seconds and kept parallel with it, as close as he dared on her doomed course.

"Olasia! Stop blubbering! Do what I say! Link your grapple with mine!"

Olasia's cries ceased. Reaching out tentatively, her sinuous arm intertwined with the arm on Klom's sled, like two straws bending around each other, as Klom directed his own grapple likewise. Finally the two sleds seemed stoutly linked.

Klom attempted first to slowly halt their fall, and then to ascend, praying all the time the arms would not rupture or unlock.

Success!

They limped back to Dashaway.

Back in the hanger, Klom ignored the wild questions from the technicians and manager, just holding Olasia close. She reeked of a terror sweat that roused Klom's protectiveness and his ardor for her. But of a sudden, he started and released the chimera.

"Tugger!"

The race through the city streets seemed to take forever. But at last the hotel came into view.

Beyond a shattered door, Lingle lay unconscious with a burgeoning broad contusion on his forehead, the stippled stamp of a majestic attack that had happily stopped short of lethality.

Of the Book of Forgetting there was no sign.

Maevelut's Pride entered Voyle's orbital plane and then began to chase the planet at a speedy clip totally consistent with all approved planetary approaches for wavepacket vessels of its size.

95

And yet to Klom the ship seemed to be dawdling, limping along at a glacial pace solely to drive him insane with worry and fear.

Would he ever catch up to Tugger, and what would happen if he did?

His imagination (once or twice over the most recent few days, he had time to ironically consider that back on Asperna he would have said he never possessed such a thing) conjured up a hundred bad scenarios. But Klom was resolved to do his best to avoid them all.

After discovering the unconscious Lingle, Olasia and Klom had rushed him to a hospital where he was quickly diagnosed, treated and pronounced safe from any bad outcomes by a Clacker physician whose deft minuscule and majuscule claws manipulated all his instruments with a musician's grace. Leaving the Vib there still uncommunicative, Klom managed to discover through numerous inquiries the physical offices of the Dashaway agency responsible for monitoring intersystem traffic to and from the city. A bored official – a colony creature known as a Volvox, seemingly just an undifferentiated mass of viridian zooids housed in a mechanical drone body featuring a clear tank full of nourishing liquid – supplied the news Klom had feared.

The Volvox's voice issued from the drone's speaker. "Yes, a craft registered to Truth's Abstract Smile arrived and departed today, all in the space of a few hours. No destination registered."

Klom and Olasia trudged back to the hospital, and found Lingle awake.

The first words from the Vib were, "*Khun* Bravalo, I truly tried to stop that arrogant monster. Honestly, I gave my all. But he and his damn bugs were just too much for me."

"What happened, Ling? Tell me everything."

Lingle massaged the bandage on his brow thoughtfully, as if reliving the assault. "Some time after you and Olasia left, that lizard lordling simply burst into our room. He ignored me and addressed Tugger. 'Arise, Worldshifter, and follow me.' And so

Tugger did! That was when I hurled myself at the villain, and got myself swatted. I don't recall anything after that, till I awoke here."

Klom's puzzlement found words. "But back on Stratcom, Smile himself said he couldn't harm us, thanks to Tugger's protection. How did he manage to hurt you, and strike at Olasia? How did he get Tugger to leave with him?"

"Well," Lingle said slowly, "that promise of protection – words from the mouth of Smile himself, remember, and maybe he was lying for some reason – was extended to us before Tugger got two-thirds of his soul back. Maybe that made a difference. Was the sphere of protection broken by Tugger's new mental confusion? Who can say? But what do you mean about striking at Olasia?"

Klom explained what had happened on the sky sleds.

"It seems, *Khun* Bravalo, that Smile wanted you busy while he stole Tugger. Perhaps if you had been here, things might have gone otherwise. After all, the strongest bond is between you and the Book. Myself and the chimera – maybe we are just on the periphery of the magic."

"No, I can't believe that…"

Silent until now, Olasia spoke. "Maybe nothing has really changed. Maybe the magic is still working."

"What do you mean?"

"Maybe Tugger knew that by going with Smile, good things would happen, for him and us."

Klom mulled over that startling theory. "I don't see how that could be true. But I will hold onto it as a hope."

Sitting up more alertly, Lingle said, "It seems to me that Smile must have only one destination: the planet Voyle, where the third *terma* is to be uncovered and fused into Tugger's soul gestalt. I suggest we follow him. His ship has departed already. Ours leaves in just a few hours. He cannot increase his lead time on us, since wavepacket travel is invariant."

"What do you mean?"

"There are no faster or slower ships. The interstellar gradients allow only one velocity."

"I never knew that."

"You should have served aboard Retta Galaxyliners as I did for decades! The tediously familiar schedules would have drilled home that fact of basic physics! But in any case, we can arrive at Voyle shortly after Truth's Abstract Smile, right on his heels, and perhaps stymie him somehow, and get our friend back."

"But are you up to travel?"

Lingle swung his legs over the side of the bed. "Of course!" But then he winced and wavered. "At least I should be ready when the hour of departure arrives. Get that doctor back in here!"

Klom found the Clacker and explained. The physician updated his diagnostics, set Lingle up with some additional drugs via microneedle perfusive, and told Klom he would release his patient in an hour if he responded well.

Klom said, "Just enough time for us to clear out the hotel room. We'll be right back!"

The management at the hotel had already repaired the door to their room. Klom found all their gear intact and began assembling it for travel.

Olasia helped with a kind of abstracted solemnity unlike her usual post-Kedgrigorn vivacity. Klom noticed her mood at last and said, "What's wrong? Are you still shaken by what happened outside?"

"No. It's only that I feel I will be a burden to you, and endanger you when you arrive at Voyle. I realise now that I am trouble and a hindrance, vulnerable to the bad actions of that evil terabase because I am only a piece of property. I don't qualify for Tugger's protection because I am not really part of this – well, this family. The family of you and Ling and the Book of

98

Forgetting. After all, as you have said, when my lease is up, then off I go, back to my agency and a new owner."

Klom grabbed Olasia by the shoulders. She averted her face, but with his pincering thumb and forefinger gentle on her chin, he brought her gaze back to his. "No, that's not true! I only mentioned your lease originally, way back on the *Penhaligon*, because I wanted you to know you had legal rights. That I would never do anything bad to you, like Kedgrigorn did. But over these weeks – Olasia, you've become so much more to me!"

"How much, Klom?"

"This much."

Klom's passionate kiss was returned in kind. When its long duration ended of mutual accord, Klom picked up Olasia's soft slight form and brought her to his bed, where they quickly shed all clothing. Klom explored her sleek furred lines, and she in turn traced his hard and scarred dimensions. He was glad he no longer wore the ugly, offputting marks of cruft from his old job.

When she swung herself eagerly atop his primed supine bulk, Klom encompassed both her breasts with one hand and used the other the cup her rear as she straddled him.

They rocketed to a bouncing climax. At the peak, Klom's mind was flung back weeks ago, to his last intercourse with poor Sorrel. How distant that era seemed! And how different this deep bond with the chimera loomed in his life, compared to the retrospectively rather shallow and superficial affair with Sorrel. Klom could not deny that he and Sorrel had solaced each other in the dire circumstances of Shipyard life; but, he saw now, it had been very much a kind of businesslike arrangement born of daily desperation.

Olasia collapsed upon Klom's chest. She whispered, "Now I truly belong to you."

"We are all together now."

Back at the hospital, Klom found Lingle waiting impatiently at the discharge station. Trained by years of stewardship to interpret the most subtle personal cues of his clients, the canny factotum instantly apprehended the changed nature of the relationship between Klom and Olasia.

"*Khun* Bravalo, I am gratified to see that you have formalised the implicit bonds between you and Olasia which only a blind and deaf man could have ignored for so long. But now, we must put aside all such carnal and emotional ceremonies and hurry to our ship!"

The subsequent days aboard *Maevelut's Pride* had consisted of a mix of angst, erotic pleasures (when Lingle very circumspectly found reasons to visit one of the ship's salons for a few hours), and planning. And now all those threads were culminating with the sight of Voyle.

Voyle was a planet boasting nearly half a billion square kilometres of varied land mass, exclusive of its gargantuan seas: over three times the habitable area of Asperna and similar worlds. And yet due to its arcane geological composition, its gravity was only slightly higher than what humans found ideal. Such an expansive territory, Lingle conveyed, fostered a comparable wealth of divergent cultures and polities, a vibrant patchwork of societies and citizens across the big planet.

The planned point of disembarkation for *Maevelut's Pride* was the Royal Sharaine starquay outside the city of Arboleda. Unfortunately, Dustar Nitch, the marabout destined to download Tugger's *ib* from the implicate order, resided in the small town of Onfroy, in the country of Navarro, almost ten thousand kilometres distant.

"How can we get there, Ling? Quickly!"

"We can take a swift plane to the borders of Navarro, three-quarters of our journey. But after that we must travel by animal-drawn carriage."

"By all the devas, why such a primitive thing?"

"Navarro is a Supressor Enclave under the aegis of a tutelary deva. Technology above a certain level is proscribed by the deva's localised manipulation of quantum events."

Klom thought a minute. "Then Truth's Abstract Smile could not have flown directly there?"

"No. He too would have to leave his starship behind at the borders of Navarro."

"So we still stand a chance of being right on his tail."

"Yes."

"Let's hurry then!"

Since his unanticipated departure from Asperna, Klom had travelled by the tidy, secure and almost boring wavepacket vessels across many light years, all without much excitement or consideration for the distances involved. So he did not at first imagine that a short jaunt by aircraft – a modest fifty-passenger Red Outlaw floater with the clan sigils of its owner decorating the hull – would stand out as a highlight of his journey. But to his surprise, Klom discovered that the relatively antique and small-scale enterprise of air travel aroused much more anticipation and elation than crossing from star to star. The takeoff, the dwindling of structures and people and landmarks to a tiny map, the passage through clouds – everything conduced to an almost mystical thrill. Seated beside Olasia, he clutched her hand tightly throughout the flight, calming her first-trip fears with his own virginal delight.

The transit across seventy-five hundred kilometres of Voyle occupied nearly eight hours, and offered a constantly changing variety of sights and sensations. Midway through the flight, hot meals of barbecued meat – huge cuts still sizzling on the bone – and tankards of frosty ale were matter-modemed on board: standard Red Outlaw fare, apparently. Klom devoured his repast, but the more herbivorously inclined Lingle and Olasia had to request substitutions, ending up with cold beet soup.

The craft put down at the border town of Hottle. Led by Lingle, the trio immediately sought out conveyance to Onfroy. The wagon master at the bustling depot – a Warthog sporting gaily beribboned tusks – informed them that luck was in their camp: they could depart in just a few hours. They used the time to freshen up at a public spa, knowing that the two-day trip across the remaining twenty-five-hundred kilometres would not allow such niceties.

At last it came time to board the capacious, comfortably outfitted wagon (adjustable seating for all manner of rumps!), in the company of the six or seven other passengers. (Doubt remained as to the exact number of riders, since one traveller consisted of a symbiotic pairing of large host and tiny attached auxiliary being.) Their luggage was loaded, and Lingle and Olasia stepped on board. But Klom remained outside a moment longer to admire the brace of steeds that would haul them across the mossy plains of Navarro. Two enormous mould-grey millipedes on either side of a central shaft, each one longer than the coach itself, secured with harnesses and reins. Their antennae questing, they dispersed a scent that reminded Klom of the commercial composting units used in the salvage yard refectories on Asperna.

With a shouted command from the driver on his outside perch, the wagon took off with skittering speed.

The ambiance in the coach was relaxed and friendly, but conversation among the disparate strangers, even when possible, soon petered out, as each party focused on its own idiosyncratic concerns. Lingle had laid in plentiful supplies of food in a hamper packed with dry ice, so the journey was reduced to snacking and drowsing and worrying, along with some speculation.

"Truth's Abstract Smile will be deprived of his majestatics in a Suppressor Enclave," Lingle observed. "That should make our encounter a little more balanced."

"Yes, but there must still be weapons that function here. Old-fashioned things."

"You are right, *Khun* Bravalo. I had not thought of that."

"I wish we had got some guns for ourselves before we left."

"Too late now. And better not to risk running afoul of any authorities in Onfroy. We must appear the aggrieved party, which we are, not the aggressors. And surely when you get close to Tugger, he will respond to you and come back to your side without a fight."

"I hope so."

Their smooth passage across leagues of pastel sphagnum conduced towards a kind of timeless drowsiness, and the three comrades all dozed. Hours later, awaking, Klom found Lingle peering abstractedly out of the window, and asked, "Ling, why do the devas ignore our mortal world? As I understand things, each deva started out as a creature of flesh and blood before they made the phase-change jump to other dimensions. Couldn't they look down and help us once in a while? Why is Tugger the only twelvestrand who stays behind?"

Lingle gnawed at a paw nail. "Vast philosophical questions, *Khun* Bravalo, for which I have no answers. Occasionally the devas do intervene. This Supressor Enclave itself is an example of such. And of course they appear when invoked by the marabouts, for ceremonial occasions. But mostly they seem content to let us poor mundane creatures struggle on our own."

"It just doesn't seem right. If I ran the universe, I'd do things different."

"So say we all."

The first night's sunset made a riot of colour in the sky, and Olasia snuggled romantically into Klom's embrace to enjoy it. The dusk song of burrow-hens brought an accompanying plangent chorus. As night dropped with its suddenly chilly temperatures, her snuggling assumed a more practical purpose: staying warm in the unheated cabin. Klom thought back to his own days in the rude, merciless, harrowing salvage yards, deprived of all the modern comforts he had now come to take for granted as he moved across the Indrajal. How had he managed to experience so many happy moments nonetheless, as he laboured mightily with his crewmates to break apart the starliners, and, afterwards, as he revelled in the thoughtlessly carefree company of Sorrel, Airey and other friends? Would he ever know such innocent times again? Or had his expanded horizons doomed him to a future of discontent?

Dawn brought an equally colourful celestial display. Lingle portioned out devilled eggs, slices of pressed meat flecked with olive slices, and a tart green juice served in one collapsible cup that the three had to share in turn. Across the wide cabin, the family of Lammergeiers – two parents and a child – split the seal on a box of carrion so noisome that every other passenger felt compelled to hang out of the windows until the meal was finished.

The unvarying smooth pace of the millipedes and the monotonous scenery of the plains – no settlements or stands of vegetation in sight – made for a day of frustrating boredom. Klom marvelled at the way this powerful bland emotion managed to outweigh even his anxiety over Tugger's fate.

But at dusk came an exciting change.

The coach tilted forward slightly as it began to descend a long gentle slope. After craning his head out one of the windows, Lingle explained: "We are dropping down into the ancient asteroid impact crater where Onfroy is situated. We should be there soon."

Indeed, as darkness descended Klom saw the lights of Onfroy spring alive, gas-burning fixtures on streetpoles and attached to the eccentric facades of the hundreds of low buildings that comprised the town.

When the coach finally halted outside the company depot, the cessation of motion seemed alien. Klom emerged on stiff legs that had almost forgotten how to bend. His smaller companions, more able to exercise a variety of postures in the cab, seemed less rusty.

They left their luggage at the depot, got directions to the temple of Dustar Nitch, and hurried down several blocks.

The temple was dark and silent and locked tight.

Klom grabbed a passing citizen. The town of Onfroy seemed to be inhabited predominantly by a human-adjacent type of being with copper-coloured skin, whose average representatives sported a keg-like torso and extremely stubby limbs, as if formerly adapted to some high-gravity planet. Likewise, any necks were almost nonexistent, as their heads seemed to sit directly on their shoulders, obligating them to swivel their whole bodies when desirous of looking in a certain direction.

This fellow, clothed in a wide cloth-of-gold robe that made him look like a dressed-up church bell, answered Klom's question with good will.

"The inexorable Dustar is conducting some kind of baptismal ceremony in a field on the outskirts of town. He began only an hour or so ago. Just follow the Avenue of Foreshortened Ambition to its end."

"That must be the ceremony to reinstall Tugger's *ib*! We have to be there!"

Klom began to run. But after a short sprint he realised that Lingle and Olasia could not keep pace, so he dashed back, scooped them up, and raced forward again.

The margin of the town was as neatly drawn as if by an invisible fence, all buildings falling away to virgin prairie. The new unimpeded view of the starry night sky made plain that they sat at the bottom of a wide bowl. Just a few hundred metres away, a ring of torches marked the ceremony. The sound of piping wind instruments, wooden rattles and large drums floated across the distance.

Klom hurried, not even noticing the negligible weight of the friends he carried. The trodden moss disseminated a cinnamon scent.

A ring of squat Navarro spectators parted easily. Klom set his friends down on the inner edge of the circle of watchers.

In the centre of the torchlight-defined space stood the naked Dustar Nitch, a typical citizen of Onfroy whose eminence was manifested by sacred armbands and a fillet, but otherwise resembling the score of similarly naked dancers who bobbed up and down with the grace of a perpetual avalanche.

Next to the Dustar stood Tugger and Truth's Abstract Smile. The terabase lordling had indeed been forced to abandon his cloak of useful and deadly techno-mites. But he still loomed large and fierce, his attention focused on the Book of Forgetting.

Tugger was swaying in time to the music and in syncopation with the dancers! Klom was startled by his four-footed friend's display of initiative and responsiveness, unprecedented since his reincarnation.

"This must be a Dervish branch of the religion," Lingle observed. "No prayers, no machines. They intend that their dancing will put themselves and Tugger into alignment with the cosmic rhythms, and thus incline his *ib* to flow naturally back into its proper mortal vessel."

"So we shouldn't interfere?"

"No. Results could be unpredictable."

"But we have to be ready to pounce to take Tugger away from Smile as soon as the dance is over. Especially if it succeeds and he is made whole."

Olasia spoke. "Look at that big patch of shadows over there. That's as close as you can get to the action. Circle around through the crowd, and I'll position myself where the lordling will be sure to see me. Once the dance is over, I'll jump out to make a scene, and you can snatch Tugger away."

"It might work," Lingle conceded.

106

"We don't have any other plan, so let's do it."

Klom and his little factotum headed in one direction, while Olasia crept off in the opposite. In a minute, they were all properly positioned.

The musicians suddenly picked up the pace of their playing. The celebrants hurled themselves through such wilder contortions as their stolid bodies permitted. Dustar Nitch achieved some arcing leaps that seemed impossible for such a bulky package. A quivering Tugger exhibited strange oscillations of his hide from head to tail, as if an army of ants were marching up and down his spine just under the skin.

Finally, with a loud crescendo, both music and dancing ceased. Tugger's legs folded beneath him and he went down to the ground.

Olasia leaped out into the trampled circle. "You! Devil Croc! Dirty Smiler! Look! You didn't kill me!"

The haughty Gorgoid turned his face away from Tugger, to make sense of the unexpected outcry.

Klom moved faster than he had ever moved before, launching himself directly at Tugger. He almost flew through the air, incidentally dealing Dustar Nitch a glancing blow that sent the hefty naked marabout sprawling like an upended turtle. Klom landed ultimately on his knees beside his friend and threw his arms about Tugger's broad neck.

Tugger licked Klom's face, and gave one of his old dopey grins.

But before Klom could pull Tugger upright or otherwise urge his friend to run away with him, Truth's Abstract Smile had taken two big strides and, with a grip on Klom's shirt, lifted the shipbreaker entirely off the ground.

Klom had always been the biggest being in any group. Never one to use his size and strength to dominate, he nevertheless relied instinctively on having the physical power to best any opponent. But in the Gorgoid he had met his match – and more.

107

Besides simply outmassing Klom, Truth's Abstract Smile, as a sixstrand, possessed a superior physiology, right down to the cellular level: muscle fibres more potent, ligaments more elastic, bones denser and better interlaced. Held in the air at arm's length, Klom could wriggle and jab punches, but to no avail, helpless as a kitten.

The Gorgoid's breath reeked of a diet of raw meat. "I am very glad you caught up with me, you witless toiler, you undeserving fool, you annoying insect. Now you will have a few seconds of terror before you attain total oblivion. I am going to use the Book of Forgetting for his original purpose. Only his going missing delayed this rightful judgment. I and my kind are the natural rulers of this universe, superior in all ways. But thousands of species of genetically inferior beings like you have bred and spread in the trillions, dominating all the planets of creation. In our lesser numbers, we multistranders have been forced to accommodate your kind, subjecting ourselves to your foolish rules, catering to your weaknesses. But no longer. For at this moment, you will all be simply wished away by my dominant will, leaving your betters to inherit an exclusive universe."

The Gorgoid hurled Klom some metres away. The soft moss cushioned his impact. With a stifled cry, Olasia rushed to his side. Klom leaped to his feet.

Truth's Abstract Smile stood by Tugger's head. He reached down with his scaly hands and grasped the two branches of the wishbone-like appendage sprouting from Tugger's brow, a feature that Klom had always considered simply decorative or vestigial.

The pressure and silence and stillness to be found only at some nighted, kilometres-deep submarine trench reigned for an unutterable span. Klom prepared himself for an instant annihilation of all he loved, a sundering so instant that he would not even be able to mourn.

But nothing happened.

108

Truth's Abstract Smile released Tugger's tuning-fork and stepped back with a dumbfounded look.

"Dustar! Have you not restored his soul?"

Dustar Nitch had righted himself after being bowled over by Klom. He sidled over obsequiously and, taking up one of Tugger's big paws, moved the Book's compliant limb through a series of mudras that seemed to evoke evanescent golden mandalas of light in the air.

"The *ib* is present. But there is still some metaphysical deficit. I fear that this carcass, not being the original vessel, is an insufficient and imperfect host."

The Gorgoid roared his anger and kicked Tugger solidly in his belly. "Useless abortion!" The Book of Forgetting showed no anger or pain, just a mute acceptance.

Fearing that the terabase's next move might be to further savage Tugger and rip him to pieces, Klom readied himself for a futile assault on the lordling, heedless of any danger to himself.

But Truth's Abstract Smile mastered his emotions with an almost visible display of willpower. "This is ridiculous and beneath me. I have wasted too much time and energy already on this useless quest. Once that idiot Bright Tide Rising slew the original Book, all was lost. But I am not defeated. If our ancestors could make the first Book, so the savants of my generation should be able to duplicate that achievement, now that they are released from any more fantasies about an easy restoration of what was lost. Now I go. But heed my words, all of you dregs! Some day soon, you will all simply evaporate, like a nightmare from which my kind has finally awakened."

Stalking off with the ultimate arrogance that deemed them all unable to harm or stop him, the Gorgoid soon disappeared. The audience and dancers and Dustar Nitch began to disperse back home to the warrens of Onfroy.

Klom and Olasia raced to Tugger; Lingle quickly joined them. The impotent Book of Forgetting got to his feet.

Klom hugged his friend and received a slobbery kiss. He sensed an old familiar presence, for the first time since retrieving the reincarnated Tugger on Stratcom. What did he care if Tugger was powerless, so long as his individuality and sense of self were restored?

Lingle spoke. "This seems a pleasant outcome – save for one thing."

"What's that?"

"The likelihood that in the perhaps not too distant future, we shall all be rendered as if we never were, once Smile and his peers succeed in recreating their own Book of Forgetting and shifting the world we know onto another, more homogenous path."

Klom felt crestfallen. Unfair! How could his happiness be so suddenly ripped away?

"But what can we do about such a fate? We are helpless. Can't we just enjoy whatever days we have left? Maybe Smile and his buddies won't succeed."

"That is a huge gamble, *Khun* Bravalo, and not one I would care to wager on."

Olasia said, "Mount Sumeru."

Klom and Lingle could only stare at the chimera.

"Mount Sumeru. It was your original destination. The triptix you got back on Asperna pointed you there from the start. Our journey isn't over. Something awaits us on Mount Sumeru. The last part of Tugger's soul is there. Or some kind of key or answer or trigger. It must be!"

Klom felt his spirits lift. "Smile never knew about Mount Sumeru. He only learned that we planned three visits to the marabouts, and so he abandoned his greedy plot too soon. We can still win! If Tugger is restored to full powers, we can make everyone safe!"

Lingle sighed. "Assuming we can survive another two deadly days in that excruciating millipede coach!"

The wavepacket ship that carried Klom, Tugger, Lingle and Olasia to the edge station in the Mount Sumeru system was named *What Is Your Why?*, a cognomen they took to be auspicious, since it seemed to hint at the primacy of a good motivation. The liner featured an astonishing number of luxuries, which all the quartet relished, given the abuse they had suffered and the rough travel conditions they had endured recently, and the prospect of unknown trials ahead. Lingle's head wound, mostly healed, still gave him occasional twinges, which he soothed with long professional massages from one of the staff: a fellow Vib, a female named Zella, with whom Lingle instantly bonded, as refugees without a homeworld often will. To Klom's eyes, she looked identical to Lingle, but the factotum described her unique beauty and spirit in glowing terms which led Klom to suspect that more than simple massages were going on. He smiled and was glad, and actually refrained from teasing his companion, as he might have teased Airey back on Asperna in a similar situation.

Olasia, Tugger and Klom spent most of their free hours in one of the ship's swimming pools. So much clean water devoted only to pleasure filled Klom with awe. When wet, Olasia's short fur dispersed a lanolin perfume that Klom found enticing. Tugger raised waves that splashed over the pool's rim, and delighted all the children with rides. Klom could not believe that his inarticulate friend – discovered, seemingly an eternity ago and half a galaxy away, in a hidden suspensor-sac a thousand years old – had been revivified and restored to his natural state. Should they abandon their quest for a broader restoration, and just take whatever happy hours remained? Always Klom came back to the possibility that Truth's Abstract Smile had raised: wiping out all cosmic sapients that did not belong to the elite terabase clade. If there was some chance he could stop this, he had to take it, no matter what personal ease and happiness he had to sacrifice.

111

Long low conversations a-bed with Olasia, conducted after their lovemaking, confirmed this judgment and decision.

"We could never truly enjoy a moment of peace and contentment with such a fate hanging over our heads, Klom."

"Yes, you are right. But what a burden."

"A burden shared is a burden halved, Klom."

"Then with four of us together, mine is quartered!"

He scooped her up and atop his erection, and she sighed and bent down for a long kiss.

The edge station that maintained its position just outside Mount Sumeru proper hosted thousands of small ships designed to carry from one to twenty individuals down into the system itself. That fleet was impressive – especially when one learned there were thousands of identical stations spaced around Mount Sumeru. But not as impressive as the view from the observatory lounge of the station.

Klom stood at the broad, tall window and found himself wordless.

The station resided above the planetary plane, the ecliptic, and so the view was as if looking down from above onto a vast and indescribable panorama.

The nucleus of the Mount Sumeru system was a gigantic black hole with the mass of a million medium-sized suns. Its appearance was of course just a vacuity with a ring of particulate activity around it.

Arrayed in a circle around the black hole were thirty-six normally functioning stars, spaced in careful proportions.

The combined gravity of the black hole and the three dozen suns maintained their flock of planets.

Twenty-five hundred planets orbited in the innermost ring, just close enough to the suns to ensure beneficent terrestrial conditions on each world. They chased each other at a distance of a mere four hundred thousand kilometres apart. Some pairs were actually linked by space elevators.

The same was true of the next ring moving outward, also sharing the broad Goldilocks zone conducive for life.

And the next ring, and the next, and the next...

Down to Ring 400, closest to the edge station, but still within the optimal zone.

A million habitable worlds, all packed elbow to elbow, their skies hosting a constant rising and setting of their fellow orbs, at different removes and of different apparent sizes, like an endless mad parade.

Lingle broke the silence. "Somewhere down there is the last part of Tugger's ascension to the Book of Forgetting."

Klom's brain hurt. "Impossible to find."

"Let us consult an expert."

The spacious, high-ceilinged, busy offices of the Indisputable Mount Sumeru Travel Agency and Sociocultural Ephemeris was staffed by identical workers behind their desks, all of which bore a plethora of communication and information-accessing devices nearly concealing the workers. The race of each identical staff member was unknown to Klom. Each being featured a body and head seemingly composed of a stack of overlapping fleshy plates of a blue-green colour, like a tree whose growths of dishlike fungus had overwhelmed it. Eyes and manipulative organs could be seen in some of the interstices of the plates. Klom decided to think of them as the Griddlecakes.

An agent beckoned to Klom and party.

"My name, eager visitors, is Susuet. How may I assist you?"

Indicating Tugger, Klom said simply, "Here is one of our party. What can you tell us about Mount Sumeru that is relevant to him?"

A tracery of colored light enwrapped Tugger. "I have digitised your party member's physical attributes. Now we conduct a quick search.... Ah, most rewarding." Susuet rotated a flatscreen so Klom could see it. "The world of Thoshubliss hosts some beings very close in nature to your companion: the Trismolians."

113

On the screen, a savannah of orangey grasses was dotted with dozens of quadrupeds who seemed nearly identical to Tugger – although without handy referents, their size could not be precisely gauged.

Klom exchanged glances with Olasia and Lingle. Tugger was busy chewing a hole in the office carpet. They nodded.

"We wish to go there," said Klom.

"I am in ecstasy! Faster than thought, your passage has been arranged. Departure Bay one nine two seven five. May the million hurtling spheres of Mount Sumeru shepherd your every step!"

After quickly collecting their modest possessions from temporary lockers, Klom and company hurried to the designated Departure Bay. Access to their hired pinnace was through a short enclosed walkway extending out from the station. They boarded, and the ship's outer door sealed shut, the walkway unmating.

Forward-facing, rear-facing, and side-facing windows in the hull revealed the lack of any cabin for the pilot. Klom was puzzled, until a sourceless voice spoke.

"Welcome aboard the *Zada Prior*! I am your pilot, and you may refer to me by the name of this vessel. I am entirely a kiberneticheskiy, embedded in the ship. No organic brain, not even that of a terabase, is as useful or reliable as one of my kind for guiding craft through the million-world weave. You may rest assured that the failure rate for trips such as these is as near zero as possible. Now, please take your seats and we will depart for Thoshubliss."

The *Zada Prior* detached and dropped down toward the ecliptic. Ring 400 assumed greater definition, and Klom could see the line of racing planets – a spinning necklace.

"Here in the outermost ring, one orbit about the black hole nucleus – a planetary year – is completed in just four point six standard days. A year for the planets of the innermost ring is one point six days. Your destination lies in Ring 250, and so you may enjoy calculating the exact length of year there."

So far the craft had flown above the ecliptic, but now it began to drop down, and the linearly careening worlds grew larger in their endless steeplechase. Klom felt overwhelmed and alarmed.

"I will enter the system in Ring 300 and then travel from one Ring to another, just to provide some excitement for your journey."

"No, don't!" Klom yelled.

"Oh, but I insist! You must admire my prowess! Also you will more intimately perceive the intricate and perfect construction of this system, created unknown eons ago by unknown beings."

The little ship deftly inserted itself between two full-sized planets in the chain, one as close to the other as a typical moon to its primary. They stayed in unchanging relative proximity to these two worlds only for seconds before darting forward across a broad gap and into Ring 299. Then, like a demented bee looking for the perfect flower, they raced from one Ring to the next, charting a zigzag path. Planets whizzed by at breakneck speeds, seemingly centimetres away from the ship's nose and tail.

Olasia squealed, clutching Klom's bicep with both hands so hard that it hurt. Lingle had his face buried in Tugger's chest.

Finally the hazardous course of merry-go-round planets came to an end, as Zada Prior guided them into a stable relationship with one cloud-mottled sphere.

"Here we are, the world of Thoshubliss! Shall I set you down at the main port of Grelltanser?"

"Yes, as soon as you can!"

Leaving the *Zada Prior* at the city's starquay, after uttering fervent thanks to their kibe pilot that were more of a prayer of humble worship than simple gratitude, Klom tried to imagine making the return trip, but quailed at the thought. The blue sky full of zipping rising and setting spheres of various sizes and maculations, the nearby worlds of adjacent Rings, did not contribute to his confidence.

Lingle soon discovered the name and location of the territory where Tugger's Trismolian cousins lived: a nature preserve dubbed the Serenity Protectorate. A rented floater – easily operable by Klom, thanks to his experience with heavy-duty deconstruction equipment – could get them there in just a few hours of moderate and safe speed. Their luggage remained behind in secure storage.

Once provisioned and up in the air, Klom finally felt some of the tension leak out of his spine.

The trip was quick and much more enjoyable than the one by millipede coach. The interval of travel passed pleasantly, with talk and food – although always at the back of Klom's mind was anxiety and wonder about what they might find. Tugger, unconcerned, rode with his massive head hanging out a window into the slipstream, tongue lolling.

Finally, adjacent to a modest sod-house reception building, the floater settled down gently to the savannah's tall grasses, bending them underneath its flat bottom. No other visitors were apparent, although Klom did note a single-person aircar bearing a governmental seal on its door.

Klom ventured inside the official outpost alone, and returned holding a gaudy printed souvenir pamphlet.

"The ranger says we can wander freely among the herd. They are gentle and friendly. Lingle, here, read this for us."

They strolled beneath the warm multiple suns toward where Tugger's cousins congregated, about half a kilometre distant. Lingle recited as they walked.

"Ranked at a qualia level that places them just below true sapience, the Trismolian quadrupeds of Serenity Protectorate constitute the last remnants of their kind anywhere in the Indrajal. Never a prolific species, the Trismolians were exploited nearly to extinction several millennia ago, when it was discovered that their unique genetic material lent itself to easy manipulation and stacking of strands. Individual members and breeding pairs from the once-extensive herds were exported in large numbers to various strandcrafter laboratories, where hopes were high for the development of autocatalytic devacentric apptitudes. But when the various lines of research proved unfruitful, and the breeding pairs refused to procreate, interest in the Trismolians waned, and their local stocks were allowed to rebound slowly to their current levels."

Halfway to the herd, Tugger grew excited and hurtled ahead. Klom dashed after him.

Tugger proved to be half again as large as his relatives. The natives crowded around their long-lost relative enthusiastically, nuzzling Tugger and making plaintive whuffling sounds. The Book of Forgetting stood proudly, like a beneficent king, home from exile and receiving his due adoration.

"So," said Klom, "millennia ago, some sly terabase genius or team of geniuses succeeded where everyone else failed. They crafted a deva – their secret weapon, the Worldshifter – who could stay stable in our dimensions, out of Tugger's ancestors. Then they kept their creation hidden from view for future use – until he went missing."

"They probably discouraged all other researchers," Lingle suggested. "To forestall a rival. Or maybe they only succeeded by a freakish stroke of luck, never to be duplicated."

Olasia spoke. "This is all very interesting. It's fascinating to know Tugger's origin and history. But how can this help us unlock all his powers?"

Klom scratched his head. "I don't know... Lingle?"

"I am at a loss."

"Well, let's go back to the floater and think about this."

Klom turned and began to walk away, but Tugger did not follow.

"Should we try to prod him to accompany us, *Khun* Bravalo?"

Klom grinned. "No, not at all. He's safe here. Let him be."

Back at their transportation they had a meal and some drinks. The ranger, a willowy Blue Aesthete wearing mere strips of artfully arrayed ribbons, came out to inform them that the reception centre was now closing for the night, but they were welcome to stay.

Klom looked at the frantic sky, as illuminated as ever. He noted for the first time that some of the celestial sights were smeared, and recalled part of Lingle's lecture while they traveled. These distorted objects lived on the far side of the central black hole, and so had their images twisted by the intervening gravity lens of that omphalos.

"You say 'for the night?'"

"A mere term of convenience. The Million Worlds never know darkness. So the devas ordained. Enjoy your evening."

After the ranger departed in his little ship, Klom suddenly felt exhausted. He had travelled so far, endured so much since leaving Asperna and his old ordained way of life. And all without any real resolution so far. Still, he had Olasia and Lingle, and Tugger reborn.

"I'm going to take a nap," Klom announced. "Wake me if anything happens."

The period from dropping off to being jostled seemed both instant and forever. Klom instinctively shot up from the floater's reclined seat.

Olasia said, "Klom, there's some kind of commotion among the herd."

Klom instantly had the floater off the ground, and in seconds had closed the short gap with the herd. He and Lingle and Olasia jumped out.

Tugger had found a mate. He was energetically but silently topping one of the females, his forelegs draped over her shoulders, while all the other Trismolians raced about in circles, bellowing.

Before Klom could formulate a positive or negative thought about this surprise, perhaps a sign of Tugger's true maturation, the sky immediately overhead filled with a dozen hovering starships. Large and menacing, they resembled so many others that Klom had once cut to pieces.

One ship opened a bay, and a lone figure, corona'd with majestatics, arced downward.

Truth's Abstract Smile rested in the air just above their heads. He looked triumphant, yet resigned to a less than perfect victory.

"We arrive too late, I see, for it took us a while to pick up your trail, once we realised our error in letting you run loose after Voyle. I acknowledge my own mistakes in dropping you, and I will surely pay a high price. In fact, my peers insisted on accompanying me, as you can see, not trusting me to bring this unfortunate enterprise to a conclusion."

"Why too late?" Klom asked.

"Our instruments reveal everything. We cannot interfere directly with the Book in this foreordained moment. As he completes his *hieros gamos* ritual, the qualia emanating from the Book of Forgetting are ramping up to complete devahood. We have only minutes until his full ascension. And afterwards – well, as before, you and your puling affections have rendered him useless to us. His loyalty cannot be compromised. So we have no choice but to destroy him this instant, before his phase change. And we will not employ half-measures."

"What are you going to do?"

"We have already done it. We have radically accelerated the natural entropic decay of Mount Sumeru's black hole. It will evaporate in just a few seconds, destabilising everything. The Million Worlds will instantly crash. A shame, really, to destroy such a brilliantly constructed astronomical treasure, but you gave us no choice. The trillions of useless creatures who must die inspire less grief. I leave now, with no regrets."

Truth's Abstract Smile rocketed up and into his ship, and the whole fleet winked out into superluminal dimensions.

Oblivious, Tugger continued his holy mating.

As the last departing black hole gravitons that had yoked Mount Sumeru together radiated out into the void, the whole world of Thoshubliss lurched, throwing Klom to the ground.

In the sky, planets began to wobble and ricochet and collide like billiard balls on an upended table. The entire glorious orrery was coming untethered, its centripetal leash snapped.

Immense roaring winds began to build. Klom fought impossibly to his feet, using the jouncing floater as a prop.

Flat on the turf, Olasia kept a grip on Lingle with one hand, while her other clutched the deep-rooted grasses. Klom strove to reach them. Eyes incredibly wide, she opened her mouth to call his name, call for help –

The ground cracked open broadly with a noise like a giant's shovel stabbed into a child's sand castle, and swallowed both Klom's friends, wailing.

Klom took a step towards the crevasse, then stopped and turned toward Tugger.

Against all circumstances, the intercourse continued, as if Tugger and his mate were stabilised by unseen forces, a nexus of solidity.

But then the soil beneath them just seemed to evanesce, as the torso of the earth split apart.

Down went Tugger and his female into the bowels of the planet.

Klom hurled himself into the canyon.

The cleft was fully illuminated, tearing open wider and deeper with every second, as the entire Mount Sumeru system flew apart in a chaotic tarantella, millions of worlds and their satellites abandoning each other. As the air whistled past his face, Klom could see Tugger finally disengage from his mate. The two Trismolians continued to plummet separately.

Some sensation caused Klom to flail about, twisting so he could look upward.

A deva had manifested at the centre of its typical silvery distortion, but without help of any animal sacrifice or boom tube.

Klom saw within that whorl the same ineffable face he had seen back on Asperna, when the marabouts consecrated the beginning of work on the *Caution Discharge Zone*. He recalled the words he had said then.

"It's – it forgives everything."

And then, within his mind only, came a voice that was instantly familiar, though never before heard.

Klom, my friend…

Klom whipped around. Below him, Tugger had halted in midair. Beside him was his mate. And she looked impossibly gravid, belly ballooning out. All this Klom saw, before the female Trismolian vanished, leaving only Tugger behind.

Klom realised he too was no longer falling. Separated by a few metres, Klom could register every detail of Tugger's jowly grin and wrinkled hide.

"Tugger!"

Yes, you know me.

"Tugger, save us! Save the world, save the universe. Just like you once saved my arm!"

I will do all that, Klom. Except for one thing. I cannot save myself.

"No! You must!"

The universe is not safe with me in it. I inspire too much contention and greed. So I must remake creation without me – without the possibility of me. Goodbye, Klom. You were a kind companion, my only friend in this long life.

"Tugger, no!"

But then all was gone.

The tall feathery lannaught trees that shaded the scattering of modest comfortable homes around the shores of Lake Zawinul rustled in the late afternoon breezes that arose each day from the amethyst lake. From one cottage, a big man stepped out onto the porch. He called back to someone inside.

"Goodbye, Mother! You'll cook what I caught today before it spoils, won't you? Do you want me to send Lingle to help? No? All right then! Until tomorrow."

The man stepped down to the grass-edged red-dirt path and walked off, humming a tune.

He was hailed at another cottage. A lazy lounger, sitting on the porch, jumped up.

"Klom, you antisocial brute! Where is our invitation to dinner at your house?"

Klom laughed. "You were there just last night, Airey. You know you need no invitation."

"Then count on seeing us tonight as well. By all the sacred spheres of Mount Sumeru, such standoffishness could make a stranger believe that we hadn't been good neighbours for ten years, ever since the salvage yards were closed down and we were all pensioned off. How I bless the coming of the Universal Reclamation of the Indrajal. No more masters, no more suffering for such as you and I. A dream come true."

As Klom nodded and began to walk away, he heard Airey yell into his house. "Sorrel! Take off your apron, my dear, we dine out again tonight!"

As he approached his own cottage, Klom felt happy. Life was as perfect as life allowed.

From his own door, two children, a boy and a girl, ran out to greet Klom. They resembled their father in size, but with more graceful faces and limbs.

"Daddy, Daddy, wait till you see what Momma got us from the trader who came through town while you were out fishing!"

Klom hoisted his son onto one shoulder, and his daughter onto the other, and carried them inside.

Olasia came in from the kitchen, wiping her hands dry. She smiled and gave Klom a kiss.

"The children say you bought them something."

"Oh, I hope you don't mind. It's just a little pet. The trader said it was a Trisomolian pup. Very rare. But no one else on his circuit wanted it, so I got it for just a few taka."

From the bedroom of the children waddled a roly-poly quadruped, all dewlaps and bumblefeet. Klom scooped it up.

"What shall we name it, Daddy?"

Klom peered deeply into the animal's eyes. The pup licked his fishhook-scarred thumb.

"I think I have an idea."

About the Author

Paul Di Filippo sold his first story in 1977, and since then has sold over two hundred more. Together with his novels, they fill some forty-five books. He lives in Providence, RI, with his partner Deborah Newton and a cocker spaniel named Moxie.

NP NOVELLAS

An exciting new series of high calibre fiction in concentrated narratives from some of the most accomplished writers around.

#1: Universal Language – Tim Major (April 2021)

An intriguing murder mystery that pays homage to Asimov's seminal robot stories and also to the classic detective tale.

Investigator Abbey Oma is dispatched to a remote and failing Martian colony tasked with solving the murder of scientist Jerem Ferrer. The killing took place in an airlock-sealed lab, and the only possible culprit is a robot incapable of harming humans...

#2: Worldshifter – Paul Di Filippo (April 2021)

A high-octane tale reminiscent of Jack Vance at his best in its sweep and imagination, but wholly Di Filippo in its execution. When lowly shipbreaker Klom stumbles upon an active organic stasis pod deep within the bowels of a derelict ship, little does he imagine the deadly danger it represents. Klom is forced into a desperate chase across the stars as the most powerful beings in the galaxy determine to claim the secrets he has unwittingly discovered.

#3: May Day – Emma Coleman (May 2021)

Abruptly orphaned during wartime, May is forced to move to the country to live with her strict church-going aunt, who never approved of May's mum nor her heathen ways. Despite Aunt Celia's disapproval, May continues to practice the superstitions her mum drummed into her, until the one time she doesn't, at which point something dark arises and proceeds to invade her life...

www.newconpress.co.uk